KITTY KITTY
BANG BANG

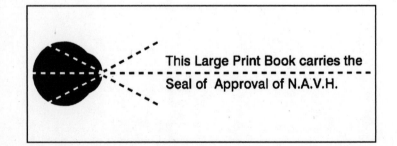

This Large Print Book carries the Seal of Approval of N.A.V.H.

KITTY KITTY BANG BANG

SPARKLE ABBEY

THORNDIKE PRESS
A part of Gale, Cengage Learning

GALE
CENGAGE Learning

Detroit • New York • San Francisco • New Haven, Conn • Waterville, Maine • London

GALE
CENGAGE Learning·

LIBRARY OF CONGRESS CATALOGING-IN-PUBLICATION DATA

Abbey, Sparkle.
  Kitty Kitty Bang Bang / by Sparkle Abbey. — Large Print edition.
    pages cm. — (The Pampered Pets Mysteries ; Book Three) (Thorndike Press Large Print Clean Reads)
    ISBN 978-1-4104-5658-8 (hardcover) — ISBN 1-4104-5658-7 (hardcover) 1. Cousins—Fiction. 2. Pet grooming salons—Fiction. 3. Cats—Fiction. 4. Pet owners—Fiction. 5. Murder—Investigation—Fiction. 6. Laguna Beach (Calif.)—Fiction. 7. Large type books. I. Title.
PS3601.B359K58 2013
813'.6—dc23   2013000517

Published in 2013 by arrangement with BelleBooks, Inc.

Printed in the United States of America
1 2 3 4 5 6 7 17 16 15 14 13

To Mary Ellen, the ultimate
cat-momma, who left us too soon.

CHAPTER ONE

"We've got to stop meeting like this," the teasing voice whispered in my ear.

The cliché would have been trite and lame had it not been delivered with such a handsome and not-at-all-lame smile. The voice belonged to Sam Gallanos, my friend, my confidant, my sometimes date.

But not tonight. Tonight I'd arrived with the esteemed Hollywood publicist, Kitty Bardot, who was my next-door neighbor and also human-mom to the famous cat-painting twins.

Now, by this, I don't mean human siblings who paint portraits of cats. I mean two cats who paint.

Kitty's Bengal cats, Tobey and Minou, to be specific.

The extravagant fete at the wonderful Hotel Montage was the launch of a traveling collection of animal art work. Kitty (the human one) was not only publicist to some of the top Hollywood stars, but also represented Mano, the Jack Russell terrier, a famous artist in his own right.

Mano had done solo exhibits in Milan, Brussels, Paris and New York. He was the headliner for this traveling exhibition, but Tobey and Minou were no slackers. The past year their art had been winning competitions, had been part of some west coast shows, and now the two Bengals had five paintings included in this exclusive event.

I looked around the room at the large canvases, full of life and color, and, well, paw prints. Kitty tells me they're abstract expressionists.

I know, I know. I don't see it either.

But back to Sam, who'd handed me a glass of champagne. "How do you think it's going?" he asked.

"Well, I think," I took a sip and answered, "the room is packed, champagne is flowing, people and checkbooks are loosening up."

Usually Kitty's partner, Franklin, attended events with her, but tonight he was under the weather, and so she'd asked me to accompany her as a favor.

Kitty had sold the idea as, "it's good to have a pet therapist in the house," but truly Tobey and Minou were so well behaved, I was more moral support than anything else.

8

I'm Caro Lamont, and though I'm a trained psychologist, my current vocation is pet therapist. I have my own business, PAWS, the Professional Animal Wellness Specialist clinic, here in Laguna Beach, California. Originally from Texas, I'd picked Laguna Beach partly because I knew the community (my family had summered here), but mostly because you couldn't ask for a more pet-friendly corner of the world. Oh, and to get away from my overbearing Texas family and the scandal created by my ex-husband. He was the reason I was no longer a practicing "people" therapist and had instead turned my attention to the more loyal species.

Grey Donovan approached from across the room. He was alone, and I have to tell you I was a bit disappointed.

"Hey there, Carolina." He gave me a hug and a kiss on the cheek, then reached out to shake Sam's hand. "Great crowd."

"I know. Who would've thought?" I looked around at the packed room.

"Mostly the curious but a few collectors," Grey noted. "From what I've heard, it sounds like there has been some big interest."

Grey owns a local art gallery. As far as I know all human artists, not dogs and cats.

Grey is also almost family.

"Where's your errant fiancée?" I referred, of course, to Melinda, my cousin who Grey was engaged to. At least last I'd heard the engagement was back on. But hey, what day is this? It could be off again.

"She and Darby had some big event at the shop." He smiled.

"Really?" It could be they really did have an event or it could be Melinda was avoiding me.

"Yeah, I think they're calling it Yappy Hour. Mel was serving drinks and pup-cakes, and Darby is taking pictures of customers' dogs."

Mel owned a high-end pet accessory shop called the Bow Wow Boutique and her friend, Darby, had Paw Prints, the pet photography studio next door.

"Sounds like a lot of fun. Leave it to Mel to come up with a brilliant marketing theme." I meant the compliment. My cousin was incredibly smart, strikingly beautiful. If it weren't for her stubborn streak . . . well, more than stubborn. Mule-headed, in fact. If not for her mule-headedness, we'd still be fast friends like we'd been as kids.

"I'm sure you're disappointed she's not here." Grey looked pointedly at the brooch pinned to the bow on the shoulder of my

10

basic black Kate Spade dress. I hadn't been certain what was appropriate attire at a pet art affair. A little black dress is always a sure fire fallback.

"I am, sugar." I smiled a smile that I have to confess was not all that sincere. "I am very disappointed."

Just then a photographer from the *Orange County News* approached.

"A picture?" he asked.

I immediately perked up. Kind of like my pooch, Dogbert, when he hears the word "walk." The idea of one-upping my cousin does the same to me.

"No problem." I quickly slid between the two most handsome guys in the room and posed for the picture — my hand lightly touching the brooch as if to straighten it.

Yes, I'm shameless.

"Thanks so much." He glanced down at the display on his camera. "A great shot. I can guarantee it will be in this week's feature article on the event."

"That will be smashing." A feature Mel was sure to see. Super!

"You're bad." Smart as well as handsome, Grey hadn't missed the significance.

"I know." My smile was much more genuine this time.

"Well, I'd better mingle." Many of Grey's

11

patrons were there, and I'm sure, like me, he felt the event was part social and part business. His gallery was very successful. I had an idea art wasn't all he did, but whatever he was involved with he'd chosen not to share, and I respected his need for privacy. He was a stand-up guy, and so no matter what the reason, I knew it was a good one.

"Off to schmooze." Grey gave me a hug and straightened the brooch. "You two girls and that pin." He shook his head.

Sam watched the exchange and also shook his head.

Grey clapped Sam on the shoulder. "Nice to see you again."

I sighed. Truly, the only way those two would be bumped out of first place for best-looking male specimens in the room was if George Clooney and Brad Pitt were in attendance, and I didn't think they were. Even if the *Ocean's Eighteen* (or whatever number they were on) duo had shown up, I'm thinking Sam and Grey would be contenders.

"So, you and your cousin are still feuding over this jewelry of your grandmother's?"

"Actually, no. Not anymore. The brooch is in the possession of its rightful owner."

"How did you get it this time? Breaking

and entering involved?" Sam's dark eyes danced.

"No," I huffed. "Her brother let me into her house. Fair and square."

"I don't know that your cousin would agree." Sam chuckled. "And I'll bet her brother is in big trouble."

I smiled, remembering how easy it had been. She'd been gone. (Granted on something pretty big, but at the time I'd had no idea.) Mitch, Mel's brother, had let me in. I kind of felt bad about putting him in the middle of things.

The piece of jewelry under discussion was a multi-jeweled basket of fruit. It had been our Grandma Tillie's. An amalgam of rubies, emeralds, and other gems in a gold basket. My inheritance from her — she'd left it to her favorite granddaughter — and to let Mel have it would mean admitting defeat. As you may have already guessed, Mel also thinks Grandma Tillie meant it to go to her.

I slipped my hand into the crook of Sam's arm. "Looks like the closing ceremonies are about to begin."

We made our way to the seating area. Virgil McKeever, the organizer and emcee, had taken the stage and was about to introduce the "artists."

As we looked for seats, I noted several clients.

Andy and Mandy Beenerman, all dressed up in designer duds and diamonds, were the center of a circle of fitness groupies. His investment business had recently tanked, but her Yoga-Pilates-Zumba studio, Mandy's Place, had taken off like a house afire. I'd helped them out with Nietzsche, their depressed and agoraphobic Lhasa Apso, a few months ago. Mandy'd also had another issue I sincerely hoped she had under control. She made eye-contact and waved in my direction.

Across the room, I'd also spotted retired newsman, Davis Pinter, one of my favorite clients. He had an adorable Cavalier King Charles, Huntley. Smart, classy. Both the man and the dog.

Tova Randall, a newish Laguna resident, was trying so hard to fit in that, well, she didn't. She was over-dressed, over-botoxed, and overly-loud.

Tova had the money, thanks to a very lucrative career as a lingerie model. She had the house, a multi-million dollar abode in the hills, thanks to the aforementioned money. She had the looks, thanks to good genes and several hours a day at Mandy's Place.

But like a new pooch who's not accepted by the pack, the rich and famous in the exclusive community still treated her like an outsider. She'd asked me to work with her and her Yorkipoo, Kiki, but when I'd arrived at her house, she'd gone to the spa. There was a message. She'd left Kiki with a dog-nanny and told her to work with me. I left a message explaining that's not how it works.

Then she'd sued my cousin, claiming Kiki'd gotten fleas at Mel's boutique. I think it all got sorted out, but it didn't matter, I was done with her. No one is allowed to pick on my family.

Except me.

There were also a lot of people from the Laguna Beach art community in attendance. I recognized a few whose paintings hung in Grey's gallery. The place was completely packed. I hoped we could find seats.

At the end of an aisle, a handsome young artist, who I'd seen talking to Kitty earlier, sat with his arms folded and his legs extended. There were some open seats just beyond.

"Excuse me. If we could just slip past you." I touched his shoulder.

He flipped longish dark hair out of his face and glanced up. His aquamarine eyes were

15

red-rimmed, and he covered his mouth with the silk scarf that accented his tux.

"So sorry." He stood to let us through and then slumped back down as soon as we'd passed.

I settled in my seat and then leaned past Sam and said, "I don't believe we've met, but I've seen you at Kitty's house. I live next door. I'm Caro Lamont."

"Clive." He nodded in our direction.

Apparently like Cher or Seal or uhm . . . Liberace, he didn't have a last name. I was kind of glad he didn't offer his hand as I wasn't wild about catching whatever he had.

"Nice to meet you, Clive."

"Allergies?" Sam asked.

Ahh. So he might not be contagious. I hadn't thought of allergies.

As usual, Sam was more observant than most. He had this incredible charismatic gift with people, and I loved him for it. Unfortunately so did all of the eligible (and some of the not actually eligible) females in Laguna Beach.

"Yes." Clive dabbed his eyes with his scarf. "I'm allergic to cats."

"Tough evening, then," Sam noted.

"Yeah." He nodded.

His date came back just then with some

cheese and dog and cat shaped crackers on a plate.

"You know I'm lactose intolerant," he snapped at her.

The girl popped a piece of the cheese in her mouth and stomped off.

Allergic to cats, can't eat the hors d'oeuvres, now his date had deserted him. The guy was not having a good evening.

The lights dimmed, and the emcee acknowledged the patrons of the event. We all applauded at the appropriate times. And then the artists themselves began to take the stage. There was Mano and his human, a large bulky guy who looked more like a WWF wrestler than a dog artist enthusiast. A couple of more canine artists, and then they shifted to make room for the cats.

Kitty looked stunning in a coffee-brown sequined Michaels Kors that shone in the light of the chandeliers and perfectly completed her cats. Their tabby rosette-dappled fur was shiny and rich. They looked out at the crowd with an aloofness, like they knew they were stars. Bengal cats are beautiful animals, and Tobey and Minou were regal representatives of the breed.

And clearly, very talented felines. Their paintings received high acclaim, rivaling Mano who'd had top-billing in the past.

Kitty now had her work cut out for her with her own cats as clients.

I made eye contact with Sam's dark eyes and could see he was as amused by the whole surreal affair as I was. We were, at that moment, in tune with each other, like a close harmony. Yin and Yang. Like peanut butter and jelly. Like milk and cookies. Chips and salsa. I suddenly remembered I'd missed eating in my rush to not make Kitty late for the festivities. I wondered where that guy's date had gone with the cheese and crackers.

Sam reached over and took my hand. His thumb stroked my wrist, and I felt a tingle in my stomach that had nothing at all to do with having missed dinner.

The lights came up, and as we stood Kitty approached from the stage area.

"Hello, Samuel. How nice to see you again." Kitty never forgot a name or a face. It was part of what made her so incredibly good as a publicist. She made connections effortlessly.

"Caro, I need a huge favor." She seemed a little breathless. I guess the excitement was quite a high, even for someone who mixed with big stars on a regular basis. I imagined this was probably more personal.

"Sure. What do you need, hon?" I was

struck by how tiny she was. Of course, I'm tall, so a lot of people seem short. But Kitty was undeniably petite. Short in stature but definitely high in energy.

"I hate to impose, but I've had something urgent come up, and I must take care of it right away."

"No problem. Don't worry about me. I can find a ride home."

"I can take Caro home," Sam volunteered.

"See?" I patted her arm. "No problem."

"I'm afraid it's more than that." Her voice shook a little, which made me wonder about her emergency. "Would you be able to take Tobey and Minou with you? I hate to ask and wouldn't if this weren't so pressing. I'll be home in less than an hour. If you could, just take them in the house and let them out of their carriers."

"No problem," Sam and I answered at the same time.

"Thanks so much, you two." She handed me her house key, relief evident on her face. "I owe you. I've got my two fur babies in their carriers backstage, and I'll let Virgil know you're taking them for me."

Kitty disappeared into the crowd. I couldn't imagine what type of emergency a Hollywood publicist might have, but I knew Kitty dealt with some pretty high-profile

19

clients. Probably some wardrobe malfunction or shoplifting scandal or meltdown captured on camera. Whatever it was, it was obviously important to the client — and to Kitty.

Sam and I made our way behind the dais and located the two cats. Tobey scolded us a bit, but Minou was calm or maybe just exhausted by her big evening. Bengal cats have a high-pitched meow, almost a squawk. In fact, about the same sound a squeaky dog toy makes. Something to think about if you're considering one of these beautiful felines as a pet.

We got the cat carriers secured in Sam's Ferrari and headed north on Pacific Coast Highway to Laguna Beach proper.

As we neared the downtown shops, traffic slowed to a crawl. Once we turned the curve at Blue Bird Canyon we could see why.

There must have been a bad accident on the highway. There were flashing lights from police cars and emergency vehicles. Orange County rescue pulled around the line of cars and stopped, EMTs piled out.

We inched forward as one of the uniformed officers began directing traffic down a side street. As we neared the intersection I could see the late model BMW, its front end nearly destroyed by the light pole it had careened into.

I suddenly felt sick.

I knew that car.

My heart thumped in my chest, and I fought to keep control. A few hours earlier I'd been in that car.

"Sam, stop." I finally choked out the words.

He jammed on the brakes, and I jumped out and hurried toward the accident scene. I wouldn't get in the way, but I had to be sure.

As I got closer, I knew. It was Kitty's car. The vanity license plate "StarPR" confirmed it. I ran faster.

CHAPTER TWO

"We've got to stop meeting like this."

Wow. Déjà vu all over again, right? Except this time the one delivering the line was Laguna Beach police detective, Judd Malone. No less handsome, but much less playful.

"What the hell are you doing, Caro?" He grabbed my arm and turned me away from the scene.

A little empathy and kindness wouldn't be out of line.

Just as soon as I had the thought, I took it back. If he were nice, there was the distinct possibility I'd lose it. My job is handling pet problems day in and day out, not dealing with life and death. The pets I work with just want to be understood, and the people I work with just want their pets under control.

"Caro?"

I guess I must have been standing there staring over Detective Hot-Shot's shoulder while I sorted out the psychology of the moment.

"I don't know. We were driving by. I recognized the car as my neighbor's. I thought I should stop and see if she was okay."

Malone crossed his arms and waited for me to continue.

I swallowed hard and searched his face. "She's not okay, is she?"

"She's not. She has very serious injuries. And, Caro, there's nothing you can do here to help." He laid his hands on my shoulders. I resisted the urge to bury my face in his solidness.

"It's best for you to go on home." He turned me away from the accident scene.

"I have Tobey and Minou," I blurted, facing him again.

"You have who?"

"Her cats. I have her cats and her keys."

"Wait. You were driving around with her cats?"

"No, no. We were at an art exhibition at The Montage, and Kitty asked me to take her cats home because something had come up. Something urgent. It seemed strange, but then the whole evening was strange with dogs and cats. Ones that paint, I mean. And Kitty would never leave her cats, but she did, so it must have been really urgent . . ."

Several emotions crossed Malone's face, and I could almost see his brain synapses trying to decide which line of questions to follow.

"Detective?" An accident scene tech waved from a few feet away.

"Be right there." He nodded to the young woman and then turned back to me. "Go home. Take the cats and go home. Don't go into Ms. Bardot's house. Stay at your house."

"Okay, but . . ."

"No, Caro. No buts. Go home."

Well, hell. I knew there wasn't anything I could do here, but what a darn helpless feeling.

I made my way back through the crowd to Sam. We walked further down PCH to a parking lot where he'd left the Ferrari. Tobey and Minou, distressed over being abandoned in their carriers, were vocal with their displeasure. Again, that crazy Bengal squawk. They were not happy kitties.

Sam held the door for me, then walked around and slid into the driver's seat. He waited a moment before starting the car.

"A bad accident?"

"Yeah. Poor Kitty. Such a great evening, then it ends like this. I hope she's going to

24

be okay. I explained to Detective Malone that I had Tobey and Minou and Kitty's keys. He asked that I not go into her house."

"Detective Malone?" Sam started the car and put it in gear. "A homicide detective? At a car crash?"

"That is strange, isn't it?" I guess I hadn't thought about the fact that Malone was at an accident scene.

It took us a while to get out of the traffic jam created by all the on-lookers, rubber-neckers and people just trying to get through. Once out of the mess, Sam headed the Ferrari toward my place.

As soon as we turned onto my street, I could see a Laguna Beach police cruiser parked in the driveway next door. I guess they figured there would be members of the media coming around, as Kitty was pretty well known in Hollywood circles.

Sam helped me with the cat carriers. As soon as we got inside, I released Tobey and Minou from their cages. They roamed the room checking things out.

Dogbert, my rescue mutt, loped down the hallway and sniffed but didn't seem too interested in our new guests. He looked up at me as if to say, "How long are they staying?" and then back at them as if asking exactly what species they were.

"Will your cats be okay with them?" Sam asked.

"I think so. We'll find out shortly."

Thelma and Louise, my cats, leapt down from where they'd been perched on my bookcases. I think they imagined themselves very well-read felines. Thelma approached Tobey, sniffed and then hissed in his face and walked away. Louise performed the same ritual with Minou, complete with arched back and don't-mess-with-me ears. Then the two walked away with a swish of their tails and strolled into the kitchen for a snack.

Wow, I think my cats might be "mean girls." I was shocked at their lack of hospitality.

"Not so wild about having company, huh?" Sam chuckled.

"Apparently not. Maybe it will just take a little time." I reached down to pet Tobey, who seemed unfazed by the exchange.

"That hissin' thing was really rude," I called to my two felines.

"I'm sure it will get better." Sam knelt to scratch Dogbert's neck. Sam was a favorite with Dogbert, since Sam could always be counted on for a ball toss or a tummy rub.

"I sure hope so. If Kitty's hospitalized for a while I may have to call in some help." I knew Don Furry at the Animal Rescue League would fill in if need be. He'd love the opportunity to get to know a couple of Bengals.

"I don't mind cat-sitting or dog-sitting for friends in a pinch, but taking care of celebrity cats is a whole different enchilada." I immediately thought of my cousin, Mel, who'd been named the guardian of Fluffy, an Emmy-winning pooch, a month or so ago. Word was it hadn't been exactly a walk in the dog park.

"I wonder if Kitty is the one who works with them on the paintings or if it's someone else," Sam mused.

"To tell you the truth, I don't know. Really, until Kitty started talking about this big event, I had no idea her cats painted." Like Sam, I was fascinated by how the process worked.

"I'm sorry, Sam. I'm a terrible hostess tonight. Would you like something to drink? A coffee or tea? A glass of wine?"

"No thanks, *hriso mou.*" Sam leaned in and kissed my forehead. Sam's Greek, and so he often lapses into his native language. I didn't know the words, but the tone told me it was an endearment. Sometimes I asked for the translation. Other times, like now, I just enjoyed the moment.

27

"It's no trouble."

"It's been a big night for you. I'll let you and your zoo here get settled and hopefully get some rest. You'll call me if you need anything?"

"I sure will, sugar." I walked Sam to the door and then locked it behind him. The police cruiser was still in the driveway next door, I noted.

I turned back to the roomful of four-legged friends. All looked at me expectantly.

"All right," I said. "Let's set some rules here. No biting, no scratching, no hissing. Be respectful of each other's space, and let's all just get along."

They looked willing.

Too bad it hadn't been that easy with some of the beauty pageant contestants I'd been in competitions with back in Texas. Whether it was Miss Texas or the Cattle Queen of Dallas County, every pageant was cutthroat, and it was pretty much always a catfight.

Chapter Three

It really was a sense of déjà vu this time.

After my lecture on the rules to my room-mates, I'd changed into my comfortable yoga pants and a PUP (Protecting Un-wanted Pets) T-shirt, brewed a cup of chamomile tea and settled into one of the easy chairs to read a book. When out of nowhere — bam, bam, bam!

I recognized the knock. Loud, I-am-in-charge knock. The man never could seem to get the concept that I had a doorbell.

Getting to my feet, I hurried to the door. Okay, I admit I didn't go there directly. I did a quick check in the hall mirror just to make sure I was somewhat presentable. Nothing to be done about the yoga pants and T-shirt, but I fluffed my hair a bit. Oh, and I might have applied some lip gloss.

Bam, bam, bam!

"Okay, okay, I'm coming." I unlocked the door and yanked it open.

Detective Judd Malone didn't wait for an invitation, he came on in. His usual uniform of jeans, dark T-shirt, and leather jacket was no surprise. I imagined that was what he'd had on at the accident scene. I'd just been too shook up to notice at the time.

"Hello, Detective."

He looked past me. "Are those your neighbor's cats?"

I nodded.

"What kind are they? They're huge."

"They're Bengal cats. Bengals are a hybrid. A cross between a domestic cat and an Asian Leopard Cat. It's a relatively new breed. Most have . . ." Malone's face said TMI. Fair enough, more info than he'd been looking for.

"I imagine you know I'm here about Ms. Bardot?" Malone was suddenly all business.

"Yes." I held my breath and hoped for good news.

"Caro." He paused. "She didn't make it."

"She —" I felt my throat close, and I swallowed hard trying to get control of my emotions.

"Are you okay?" Malone's voice was softer than I'd ever heard it. At least when addressing me.

I gulped and closed my eyes. I could sense him waiting. Waiting for me to process what he'd just told me. Waiting for me to regain control. Waiting for the questions he knew would eventually come.

"Too many injuries?" I finally asked. Whatever her emergency had been, it had seemed to upset her. She'd been shaken, and Kitty was never shaken. I remembered her voice as she'd asked me to take care of Tobey and Minou and get them home. The cats. What would happen to the cats now? "Was she going too fast?"

"Not exactly." Malone's voice was serious and grim. "We won't know until we have a lot more information from the crime lab. It's too soon to tell, but it may have been a case of road rage. Kitty Bardot was shot."

"Shot?"

To say I had trouble getting to sleep after Malone left would be an understatement. He'd admonished me to lock my doors and not answer any questions if the press came knocking or calling. He seemed to think they would.

I got ready for bed, but after an hour of tossing and turning, I finally gave up, moved to the living room, and switched on the television. Maybe a late night movie would turn off my racing thoughts.

But I'm afraid even my usual favorite classic movie channel couldn't complete with trying to figure out how my neighbor went from top of her game, enjoying her life, to gone.

I wondered about road rage, and though I'd dealt with some clients with anger and impulse control issues, it was a big step to go from irritation to rage. A big step to go from, I want to pull in front of you and pay you back, to I want you to die.

And, of course, there was the huge step of carrying a weapon to actually pointing a gun at another human being and pulling the trigger.

The cases across the country where there'd been sniper incidents rolled around in my brain too. I hoped it wasn't road rage, but I also hoped it wasn't a random shooter because of the larger danger to the whole community.

And, because I have this curiosity (I think Malone might have called it nosiness) I wondered how the police were going to sort out what had actually happened. Pacific Coast Highway was a busy place even as late as the shooting had happened. Maybe someone saw something. If so, I prayed they'd come forward.

Whoever shot Kitty had ended a life, and I had every confidence Malone and his colleagues would track down the killer. I only hoped it was soon.

CHAPTER FOUR

By the time I finally fell asleep, there was nothing on but infomercials. The last thing I remembered was some thermal pants promising thinner thighs. It was no wonder I woke up with my brain foggy and my neck stiff.

I turned on the television and flipped it to a news channel as I brewed my morning coffee. Kitty's death was the lead story on every station. Both local and national news.

I listened as veteran anchor Tom Patron and newbie Maggie Rameriz reported the incident. There was no comment from the Laguna Beach police department, but knowing it wasn't a simple accident, I listened for any clue about what had really happened.

The Bengal cats were agitated this morning. As were Thelma and Louise. Dogbert, bless his little doggie heart, was an observer in the kitty-cat chaos, trying to figure out what was up.

I got dressed and checked the messages at my office. Nothing urgent. Only a potential new client with an out of control Chihuahua, who'd been referred by Diana Knight. Diana's one of my best friends in the entire world, and I had plans to meet her for a late lunch. In fact, if I were going to get everything done and make our lunch date, I'd better get going.

I volunteer one day a week for four hours at the Laguna Beach Animal Rescue, and this was my day.

The bright SoCal sunshine was blinding as I backed out of my garage. The cloudless blue sky offered the promise of another beautiful fall day, and I was reminded again of why I'd chosen to live in Laguna. As I pulled my vintage Mercedes convertible out and hit the button to close my garage door, I noted the police cruiser still parked in Kitty's driveway next door. A few news people had collected across the street. Only a couple of local stations' vans and a handful of freelance reporters. Probably more were at her agency office and still more at the police station. I was certain Malone could handle them.

Thank goodness they had no interest in me. I headed into the Village area and made a quick stop at the Koffee Klatch for a caffeine pick-me-up.

Verdi, one of my favorite baristas, was on duty. She always took care of us regulars, somehow remembering what we all ordered, and she also maintained calm and patience when things got crazy during tourist season.

"Hazelnut latte, sugar-free," she called back to the young man behind her. "Good morning, Caro. How are you today?"

"I'm all right," I answered. "How about you?"

"Looking for a job, I'm afraid." She pushed burgundy hair off her forehead with a hand that held more rings than I'd ever seen on one hand.

"Oh, no." I was shocked. Verdi truly was one of the best workers they had. "Is the Koffee Klatch cutting back?"

"No, I only work here part-time. My other job is the problem. I also work at Purple Haze and by the end of next week they're closing."

I recognized the shop as being a retro clothing store that'd been in town for many years. A sign of the times, I'm afraid. Many of the local retailers had been hurt when the real estate bubble burst.

"Oh, sugar, I'm so sorry." I took my coffee from her. "I'll sure keep my ears open for any possibilities."

"Thanks, Caro, I'd appreciate it." Verdi handed me my change and moved on to the next person in line. Definitely multi-tasking was one of her talents, along with her great people skills. I wished I knew of someone in the market for someone like her.

I'd have to ask my friend, Walt Cambrian. Walt was the local blogger, photographer, and resident grumpy-old man. And as one of life's great observers, he somehow managed to know everything about everyone.

Speaking of which, I'd have to see what Walt knew about Kitty and this whole road rage theory the police had. Kitty was a powerhouse, and I could see if she drove the way she did everything else, maybe she had gotten crossways with another driver. Still, what was the world coming to where aggressive driving resulted in shots being fired instead of just middle fingers being lifted?

I took my coffee and slipped out the front door. I'd come the back way through the village streets to get to the Koffee Klatch and had avoided the section of Pacific Coast Highway where Kitty had crashed. But I had to drive past it as I turned north to connect with Laguna Canyon Road.

Her car was gone, thank heaven, but there

was still debris scattered around the area and accident scene tape stretched across some barricades. There was a crew working on repairing the light pole, and a few onlookers stood talking nearby.

The road out of town to the ARL was pretty deserted at this time of day. I'd missed the early morning commuters headed to the freeway and parts either north or south. I turned into the lot and parked my car.

Just as I opened the car door, my phone beeped. I glanced at it. It was my mother, Katherine Lamont. "Mama Kat" to me. I couldn't imagine she'd made the connection between the news stories about Kitty and me so she must just be calling to harangue me about . . . well, about many things. Let's just say she had her opinion about how I ought to be living my life and I had mine.

I'd call her back later.

I hoped Don Furry, a friend and one of the most dedicated workers at the ARL, was on duty. He knew a lot about cats, and I wanted to talk to him about caring for Tobey and Minou in case I needed to keep them for a bit while things were being sorted out.

As I stepped inside the front door, I spotted Don, who led a Chow-Labrador mix to the exercise area. More Chow than Lab. The dog clearly needed the exercise as she was over-excited. She pulled at the leash, barked and twirled. The dog continued her dance until she'd wrapped the leash around Don's legs.

I quickly got alongside Don and helped him get untangled from the leash. I knew he was capable and could've handled it, but it was easier with two people.

"What's this girl's story?" I asked as we continued toward the exercise area.

"The owner dropped her off. Seems he and his wife are getting divorced and neither one will be living in a place where pets are allowed," Don explained.

"Man, what a shame." I shook my head in disgust. Too often pets were caught in the middle of life changes. Divorce, job changes, relocations, or cases where the would-be pet owner thought they wanted a pet, and then reality set in. You'd be surprised at the number of cases where the pet owner simply didn't do their research about what was involved with taking care of a dog or cat. Or a bunny or turtle. Right now the Laguna Beach ARL had several of each.

Sorry for the lecture. The unfairness of it for the animals just gets my dander up.

I got out some of the toys and balls while Don let the dog into the exercise pen.

"There you go, Zilla. Wear yourself out." He turned her loose.

"Zilla for Godzilla?" I asked. The beautiful dog didn't really look like a Godzilla, but you never knew what reference pet owners would pick.

"No, Zilla, because apparently the dog was a wedding gift, and the bride was such a 'Bridezilla.' Big surprise the couple's divorcing, huh?"

We took turns throwing tennis balls for Zilla, and I filled Don in on my situation with Kitty's two cats. He'd heard about the accident but didn't mention anything about the road rage theory, which to my knowledge still hadn't been publicized. Malone hadn't asked me to not talk about it, but I didn't feel right spreading the story when it might be no more than theory.

"Bengal cats are often nocturnal, so don't be surprised if they roam around the house at night," Don told me. "Other than being night creatures and pretty active, the only other thing I know about them is unlike most felines, they love water. You may want to keep an eye on the fountain in your living room."

"Good to know." I thanked him and went

back inside to help with some dog baths.

By the time my shift was over, I was covered with dog fur, and my jeans were soaked from sudsing down a Great Pyrenees the size of a pony. They are superb herding dogs, very affectionate and gentle, but this one weighed more than me. Daniel, the shelter's vet, had him on a strict diet, but even when he got down to a healthy weight he was going to be one big fella. He'd been found wandering and wasn't micro-chipped, so the shelter volunteers were trying to get the word out about him in hopes of locating his owner. In the interim, they were calling him Lord Rawnsley. A reference, I imagined, to the Rawnsley estate in *Those Magnificent Men in their Flying Machines.* Most of the Laguna Beach volunteers not only knew pets, they also knew movies.

Rawnsley very much needed to get some exercise, and the exercise pen was not going to cut it for him. I promised to stop by later in the week and take him on a field trip to the dog park if he hadn't been adopted.

I'd worn jeans and a lace T-shirt. The jeans were a good idea, the lace T-shirt not so much. I would have just gone on to my lunch with Diana if I hadn't been so bedraggled. Since I'd been Rawnsleyed, I decided I needed to stop by home.

41

As I pulled into the driveway, I noted not much had changed next door. Still the cruiser. I didn't know if it was a different one or the same. The news vans across the street didn't look like they'd moved.

I left the Mercedes in the driveway, quickly unlocked my front door and slipped in, not wanting to invite any interest on the part of the reporters and paparazzi.

The door shut behind me with a click, and I paused for a moment and then started to call out a hello to my animals.

The sight that greeted me left me speechless.

Oh. My. God. My house had been ransacked.

Books were pulled off the shelves. Vases and knick-knacks were smashed on the floor. The drapes to the patio door hung at an angle. Lamps were tipped over. The family pictures that had adorned my mantle were askew, some on the hearth.

Shock paralyzed me for a moment. My first thought was my animals. I didn't care what the thieves had taken, but if they'd hurt my pets, I would be coming after them.

"Dogbert? Thelma? Louise?" I called to my animals and stepped around a Waterford crystal candleholder that lay at my feet.

The effort seemed more like vandalism than theft.

"Well, for cryin' in a bucket, what were you looking for?"

I said the words aloud and suddenly hearing my own voice in the silence, realized the thieves could still be in the house.

I reached in my handbag for my cell phone and dialed 911.

"Dogbert?" I called.

No answer from Dog. Now I was really shaken. What if they'd taken him?

"What's your emergency?" The Laguna Beach PD dispatch answered, and I suddenly remembered I had other fur-kid guests. What if someone had been after Kitty's artist Bengals?

"Someone has broken into my house," I told the voice.

"Have you entered your home?" he asked.

"I'm inside." I could hear him give some sort of a code and assumed he was communicating with LBPD officers on duty.

"Ma'am, get out of the house. Please go outside and wait in your car for the officers to arrive. We're sending someone right now."

"Okay," I said and hung up. No way was I going back outside until I was sure my pets were all right. If the bad guys were still in the house, well, they would have to deal

43

with me.

I picked up the crystal candlestick from the floor and felt the weight of it in my hand. Not a bad weapon. I could do some serious damage if I needed to. I crept down the hallway.

"Dogbert?" I called. "Thelma, Louise? Tobey, Minou?" I heard a faint whimper from behind the couch.

Lifting the big quilt I usually kept draped on the back of the couch, I could see my poor dog had managed to get lodged between the wall and a pile of books that had been pulled from my bookshelves. I moved the books and got him out.

"Are you okay, boy?"

He barked in answer then growled, then barked again. Suddenly Tobey and Minou shot through the room follow by Thelma and then Louise.

Well, okay. All fur-kids accounted for.

Minou stopped in her tracks when she saw me. Thelma ran back and hissed at her. Tobey circled and growled deep in his throat. Not to be outdone, Louise arched her spine and hissed too.

By this time Dogbert had decided to hide behind my legs. I could feel his little body leaning against my calves.

"Come on, you guys. It's okay." I moved

toward the cats who were obviously spooked by the whole ordeal.

The doorbell chimed, and then there was a knock. "Police."

At the sound, Thelma jumped on the bookshelves, knocking the rest of the crystal in a heap. Louise climbed up the front window drapes using her claws and perched on top of the half-wall separating my living room from my dining room. And Tobey, in one beautiful leopard-like movement, pounced and landed in the middle of my couch which sent the one remaining cushion shooting up. As if in slow motion, it was airborne and then tumbled end over end and landed on the only remaining upright lamp, which in turn fell with a crash.

"Ma'am?" I turned to look at the uniformed officer who stood in my entryway.

Then I turned back to survey the mass destruction that used to be my living room, and suddenly knew the damage was not the result of an intruder.

My home had been vandalized by four felines.

Once I'd explained to the very nice officer about the confusion and assured him my home had not really had a break-in, I started cleaning up the mess and called Diana to let her know I was going to need to reschedule our lunch. Then I placed a call to Detective Judd Malone.

If this was the result of only one day of cohabitation, keeping Kitty's two cats at my house was not going to work out. Tobey and Minou needed to be in their own home.

Detective Malone called me back right away and gave the go ahead to move them to Kitty's. He even said he'd call the officer stationed in her driveway and let him know I would be bringing the cats over.

I looked around the room. I'd managed to pick up most of the broken items and had made a pile of those I thought could be salvaged.

Dogbert was sound asleep in his bed, Thelma and Louise sunned themselves in the sunlight streaming through the patio door, and Tobey and Minou were curled up sound asleep on a soft blanket in a corner of the room.

Demolition work is tiring.

CHAPTER FIVE

Tobey and Minou were happy to be home. After first exploring the house and probably, truth be told, looking for their human mom, they had settled in.

It had been two days, and still no word about who might have shot Kitty. But the cats and I had developed a regular routine. The police cruiser was gone from the driveway. I always came in through the back so I didn't attract any of the reporters who were still stationed across the street.

I located Tobey and Minou's cat food in the pantry and filled their bowls. It still seemed odd being in Kitty's house without her there. I'd been in the living room many times and on the enclosed veranda, which was set up for Tobey and Minou, but in all the years we'd been neighbors, I'd never been in the rest of the house.

The kitchen was high-class gourmet with top of the line steel appliances and gleam-

47

ing marble countertops. That wasn't any surprise, as Kitty seemed to be the type of person to whom it mattered, whether you were a gourmet cook or not.

I filled the cats' bowls with fresh water. Litter boxes probably needed checking too. They were located in a large storage area off the veranda. One labeled "Tobey" and the other "Minou." Though they were really smart cats, I was pretty sure they couldn't read. I cleaned the pans.

The two felines eyed me from their plush beds. They truly were beautiful animals. It was so much easier with them at Kitty's. They were surrounded by their own things and were much less anxious.

I'd gone through the cat care checklist in my head — fill their bowls, check their water, clean the litter pans — when the doorbell rang. It almost had to be a salesperson or someone to check the electric meter as all the neighbors knew about Kitty.

"It's okay, kids," I called to the cats as if they understood. "I'll get it." As opposed to them answering the door, I guess.

I opened the door to a woman who probably stood no more than five-foot two in her platform shoes. Over her head, I could see there was a gray-tone pickup parked in the driveway. I had this flash of big blonde hair, tiny tanned arms, neon-pink halter top and flowered capris before the pixie threw her arms around me in a bear hug.

"Kitty, thank God I've found you!" Her high-pitched voice was buried in the clench, but I was sure that was what she said.

"Uh . . . uh, I'm not. Wait." I tried to pull myself loose, but she was deceptively strong for such a little thing.

I'm tall, and I work out, but Tinkerbell had a vise grip.

I finally extricated myself and stepped back into the entry.

"I'm so sorry, but I'm not Kitty."

"You're not?" She tipped her bleached blonde head to one side. Kind of like Dogbert did when he wondered what I was attempting to communicate.

"No."

"Well, I did think you were pretty tall." She looked up at me. "But if you're not her, then who the hell are you? This is Kitty Bardot's house, isn't it?"

"It is. And may I ask who you are?"

"Well, a-course you can. I'm her sister."

Holy kitty litter, Batman.

Not the answer I expected. I didn't know Kitty had a sister, and I was willing to bet my trust fund Malone had no idea either. Although before I started gambling away

49

my safety net, I needed to remember that Detective Malone always operated on a need-to-know basis, and maybe he hadn't thought I needed to know this little tidbit.

The first thought I had was, oh-my-gosh Kitty has a sister.

My second thought was, oh-my-gosh she doesn't know her sister is dead.

"Come in. I'm afraid I have very bad news for you."

"Whatdyamean?"

"I'm Caro Lamont, and I'm a friend of Kitty's. I'm here taking care of her two cats, Tobey and Minou."

She watched me intently.

"Hon, I'm going to call the police, and they'll explain. You just come on in and sit down."

"My sister's in jail?" She followed me into the living room.

"Oh, honey, no. Nothing like that." I didn't want to be the one to break the news, but I didn't think she was going to wait until Malone arrived. I couldn't say I blamed her.

"I don't think I want to wait for the police," she said, her jaw set like a stubborn Doberman. "If you're her friend, you better tell me right now. Where is my sister?"

I took a deep breath. Better to just say it. I took her hands in mine.

50

"A couple of days ago, on her way home from an event, Kitty was killed."

"Oh, no. Do not tell me that." She pulled away from me, and her voice got louder and higher. "I have been searching for my sister for fifteen years. Do not tell me that I found her only to come here and find out that she's dead. Do. Not. Tell. Me."

The little flowered pixie twirled in circles.

"Oh, no. Oh, no. Oh, NO!" Her voice crescendoed into the loudest scream I have ever in my entire life heard. Ever.

And then — boom! She collapsed on the floor.

Chapter Six

The woman claiming to be Kitty's long lost sister finally came to. I'd propped her up against one of Kitty's fancy black velvet chairs.

She opened cornflower blues eyes that promptly filled with tears. "I'm sorry. I can't believe my sister is dead." She scooted up into the chair and flipped long frizzy blonde hair out of her eyes. "What did you say your name was?"

"Caro. Caro Lamont. I live next door," I answered. "And I didn't catch your name."

"It's April Mae Wooben. But you can call me June. Most everyone does."

I blinked. "What?" Never mind. Obviously I hadn't heard her right. We'd sort out the name thing later. "I didn't know Kitty had a sister."

"We didn't know we were sisters until recently. We were adopted when we were just tiny. Kitty was three, and I was just a baby. Our mama gave us up for adoption, and I've been trying to find her, our mama that is, and my sister, ever since I was old enough to know you could do that sort of thing. But no luck."

She stopped rambling for a moment and took a breath. Thank God. I was afraid she would pass out again from lack of oxygen.

"Then out of the blue I was contacted by this private detective. He was looking for me. He hooked me up with my sister, and we were talking about maybe meeting. I couldn't wait, so I just decided to drive on out here. She wasn't hard to find you know."

"Where are you from?" I'd glanced at the pickup truck and noticed the plates weren't California plates but hadn't looked closely enough to know where.

"Why, I'm from Eminence, Missouri. Southern Missouri. The Show Me state."

"A long trip then."

"It wasn't too bad. I figured out where Kitty lived, then I called her. She gave me her address, and here I am. But . . . but . . . I can't. Oh, Lord."

I feared we were headed for a repeat of the earlier faint so I opted to keep April Mae . . . uhm . . . June talking.

"So she was expecting you?"

"She was. What happened? It wasn't a

heart attack or something, was it? That's part of what got us looking for each other. Tryin' to figure out our health backgrounds. Now what will I dooooo . . ." The final word turned into a wail. One that had a lot in common with a police siren.

Speaking of police, I should probably alert them.

"First off let me call Detective Malone. He's the one who's investigating your sister's death."

I wasn't sure she'd heard me over the wail. I took my cell phone and stepped into the kitchen. April or Mae or whatever the heck her name was certainly was nothing like Kitty.

Kitty had always been the epitome of decorum in all the time I'd known her. Understated elegance, cultured voice, proper society manners. I was sure none of those descriptors had ever been used in the same sentence with the blonde bundle of nerves who was nearing nuclear meltdown in Kitty's living room.

The commotion had attracted the attention of Tobey and Minou who'd come to see what the noise was all about. They probably thought it was the smoke alarm. It had the same ear-piercing pitch.

"Hello? Caro?" Malone had answered,

54

and I hadn't heard him. "Is everything okay?"

"I'm fine. Can you hold on just a minute?" I stepped out onto the patio to escape the clamor.

I quickly filled him in. At least with the little I knew anyway.

"I'll be right there." And he hung up.

I dreaded going back in the house, but figured I should check on her. She had to be in shock with the news she'd just had.

I stepped inside. The house was quiet.

"Can I get you some water or . . ." The sight that greeted me was not what I expected.

April Mae or — uhm June — was curled up on the couch with the two cats in her lap. Now these two felines had only barely begun to warm up to me, and I'd been their primary caretaker and source of food for the past two days. But the little blonde sprite was apparently the Cat Whisperer and had charmed them in a matter of minutes.

Cats can sometimes be one-human animals. Loyal to a particular person and apathetic about anyone else. Maybe they somehow knew this human shared genes with their beloved owner.

She scratched behind an ear of each feline, and massive purring commenced.

April Mae smiled. "Aren't they the most gorgeous things you have ever seen? Do they belong to my sister?"

"They do." I didn't think it would be a good idea to point out that it was really past tense. "Their names are Tobey and Minou. This one is Minou, and the slightly larger one is Tobey. They paint."

The doorbell rang, and we all jumped. Malone must have been in the neighborhood when he'd taken my call.

I answered the door, and sure enough it was Mr. Serious himself. I couldn't wait to see how he dealt with April-Mae-You-Can-Call-Me-June.

When Malone walked into Kitty's living room, I thought April Mae was going to swoon again.

She looked up at him and batted her baby blues. "Well, my, my. I guess here in California even the police officers are movie star handsome."

"Detective Judd Malone, ma'am."

"My name is April Mae, but you can call me June."

He looked at me. I shrugged. I couldn't help him out; I'd not been able to sort the name thing out myself.

"And you say you're Ms. Bardot's sister?"

"I am." She went into the same explana-

56

tion she'd given me about looking for Kitty, them finding each other, and her deciding to drive to California. Then, lip trembling, she added the part about ringing the doorbell and finding me in Kitty's house. And being told her sister was dead.

Malone looked at me pointedly.

"I was here feeding the cats," I explained.

"Are you staying somewhere nearby?" he asked the little sprite as she went on petting Tobey and Minou, and they continued eyeing Malone.

I swear she looked like a little girl with a lap full of kittens.

"I'd planned to stay here with my sister." Her lip began to tremble again.

"Let me call Ms. Bardot's attorney and see if staying here is acceptable." It seemed Malone was as affected by her threatened tears as I was.

He excused himself and went outside to make the call.

It didn't take long, and he was back.

"Okay, ma'am, you'll need to give Mr. Paul Kantor a call tomorrow morning. He's Ms. Bardot's attorney. I've written his number on my card." He handed her his business card. "If anything comes up, please give me a call. As far as the reporters who are sure to be knocking on the door, I'd suggest not talking to them."

April Mae or — uhm June took the card and clutched it against her ample chest. "Like if what kind of anything comes up, officer?" The pixie had developed a Marilyn Monroe Happy-Birthday-Mr. President breathiness. Caused by hyper-aware hormones one could only guess. Malone had that effect on a lot of females.

He was oblivious to it, which made him all the more irresistible. "Anything to do with your sister's accident."

"Oh sure, you bet your bootie, officer. If anything comes up, I'll call."

Malone looked at me, started to say something, and then turned and left.

"I just love strong, silent types, don't you?" April-Mae-You-Can-Call-Me-June intoned as the door clicked shut.

"Hmmm." I was non-committal, not that she noticed. In my interactions with Malone, he'd been strong but certainly not silent. I guess I had that effect on him. Something to do with interfering in his murder investigation.

"Come on, I'll show you where Tobey and Minou's food and supplies are kept."

CHAPTER SEVEN

The next morning, I almost wondered if I'd dreamed the craziness of the previous night. But the gray splotched pickup truck with Missouri plates was still parked in the driveway next door.

I had an appointment in Ruby Point, the gated-community where my friend Diana and several of my clients lived. This was the referral from Diana.

Nicky Chang was a divorced, single, empty-nest mom with a Chihuahua who'd become aggressive with anyone who came near her. I wasn't sure if Nicky worked, or if she did, what the woman did for a living. Diana had given me none of those details, but tons of intel about the dog. With Diana it's always about the animals, not the people, and I knew she'd expect a full report when we met later for lunch.

The guard at the gate recognized me and waved me through. I had no trouble locating the house. The homes were all huge, all gorgeous, and all had million-dollar views. Nicky Chang's house had a traditional look with a stone front and walled back yard.

I rang the doorbell at the Chang house and introduced myself. It didn't take long to determine the issue with Sunshine, the problem Chihuahua. Sunny was being carried everywhere. With no walks and no effort expended to get from Point A to Point B, Sunny had loads of energy to get into trouble.

I prescribed daily walks and limiting the amount of time Sunshine was carried. The more exercise the little dog got, the better for her and I'd be willing to bet the fewer issues she would have. I also thought Nicky Chang might be having a problem with babying Sunny a bit too much, but I didn't see any evidence of that while I was there. I told Nicky I'd check back with them in a week and encouraged her to call me if she needed me before then.

It was a little slice of enjoyable normal to be having lunch out with Diana. Seemed like nothing had been normal lately. We'd finally rescheduled our lunch from the day the cats had gone wild and trashed my house, and I was really looking forward to the chance to catch up with her.

We had agreed on G.G.'s Bistro. I'd asked for a table on the patio and had just ordered an iced tea when Diana arrived. I waved to make sure Diana saw I was already there, and she waved back.

At seventy-something she still turned heads. Elegant, as always, today she wore Dior, and she wore it with style. A short-sleeved peach summer dress that complemented her blonde hair, matching peach sandals, and a large Dior quilted handbag aka doggie carrier. Not that the Dior folks meant for it to be used as a dog carrier, but Diana was hardly ever without Mr. Wiggles, her rescue puggle. Mr. Wiggles was so well-behaved you wouldn't even know he was there. He didn't make a peep as Diana made her way to the table, but I could see his little black nose peeking over the top of the bag. Many Laguna restaurants allow dogs, at least for patio dining.

"So, finally we get to have lunch." She seated herself in the chair and settled Mr. Wiggles on the extra chair.

"I know." The waitress came with my tea. "It's been way too long."

While Diana ordered her beverage, I leaned over to rub Mr. Wiggles' head and enjoyed the breeze. It was a gorgeous day, and the bistro had a wonderful relaxed ambiance.

"Oh my, you look lovely today, Caro. Lily Pulitzer?"

Diana's eye for fashion was keen.

"Why, yes it is." I smoothed the skirt of my turquoise striped sundress.

"It's a great color for a pretty red-head like you." Diana reached over and patted my hand. "I've missed you, honey."

"I've missed you too." I truly had. The woman's view of the world and down-home common sense was a breath of fresh air for me. She reminded me in so many ways of my Grandma Tillie. Though Dallas, Texas is a long way from Hollywood (and I mean that less in miles and more in the philosophical sense), Diana and Grandma Tillie would have seen eye to eye on a whole lot of topics.

Diana leaned forward and lowered her voice. "Lots of excitement with your neighbor."

"You're not going to believe the latest development." I filled Diana in on Kitty's sister's arrival.

"Caro, it's like a soap opera. The secret sister no one knew about." Her eyes were wide. "So, how's the investigation going?"

"I only know what I hear on the news."

"I meant *your* investigation, dear."

"I'm not investigating." I lowered my voice and looked around. I wasn't sure if I thought Malone was lurking somewhere or why exactly we were whispering. Probably guilt on my part more than anything.

"Sure. Right." Diana laughed. "Caro, you can't help yourself. You're naturally curious, and you're good at figuring out people. I think the Laguna Beach PD ought to hire you as a consultant."

"Not interested, and I'm quite sure one particular homicide detective would not be in favor."

"How is Detective Dreamy?" She took a sip of the Perrier the waitress had slipped in front of her.

"He's fine."

She laughed at my obvious avoidance of a discussion about Judd Malone. "So, what's this sister like?"

"Kitty's sister is uhmm . . . an interesting character."

"How so?" Diana opened her menu. "Do you really think this woman is her sister? Is she nice?"

"She's not at all like Kitty." I glanced down at the menu I held, vacillating between a salad or a kabob. "But I do believe she's Kitty's sister."

"What about Ms. Bardot's cats?" Diana tapped manicured nails painted a shade of peach just slightly deeper than the color of her dress. The lady was always put together well. "Are you still taking care of them, or is this sister the caretaker now?"

"She is, and she's wonderful with Tobey and Minou. They definitely have taken to her."

"Sometimes animals read people better than we do. Poor thing. Here she finally finds her sister and then loses her before they can meet." Diana sighed. "So sad."

The waitress was back, and we ordered. I'd decided on the grilled calamari salad, and Diana picked the Alexander kabob. I was sure Mr. Wiggles would love the beef. The bistro was casually decorated, a tasteful but comfortable décor. I felt myself relax as I explained (read unloaded) to Diana how I felt about Kitty's sudden death and then finding out she had this secret.

"I guess you can live next door to someone and never really know them," I mused, stirring my tea. "Kitty wasn't secretive, but we mostly talked about our yards or our pets. We exchanged house keys and kept an eye out for each other's houses if one of us were out of town. But I guess I didn't really know her at all. We were both always so busy."

"I liked Kitty Bardot, and she was a fierce advocate for her clients, but I use Octavia Berns as my publicist." Diana sipped her Perrier. "Octavia and I have been together for years, and she gets me. I'm afraid Bardot and Company would've pushed for more than I'd like to take on at this stage of my life." Diana slipped a bread crust to Mr. Wiggles. "Still, they seemed to be the up-and-coming firm."

"That was my impression too."

The waitress arrived with our entrees, and we waited until she'd left to resume our conversation.

"Caro, I need to ask you for a favor."

"Anything, Diana."

"I'm going to Italy with Dino. I've never been, and this seems like a perfect opportunity."

"Taking you home to meet the family?" I teased. Diana and the local restaurateur, Dino Riccio, had recently been an item.

She ignored my comment.

"I can't take Mr. Wiggles and the rest with me. I wondered if you'd stop by the house a couple of times during the week to check with Bella and see how she's doing with the crowd." By crowd, Diana meant her other assorted animals.

Diana had a beautiful Maine Coon cat,

Gypsy, Mr. Wiggles, her lop-eared puggle, Barbary, her grumpy one-eyed basset hound, and Abe, her goat. All rescues. As well as assorted other cats and dogs she fostered. At one point, I believe she also had a rooster, Walter. Though I think Walter had now been adopted by a very nice family.

"Also, would it be okay if I gave Bella your phone number to call if she runs into any problems? I know she'll do fine, but I'd feel better if she had someone she could contact."

"Absolutely, no problem."

We walked out together, and I walked Diana to her car, kissed her on the cheek and wished her well on her trip to Italy. I was so excited for her. With Diana on her way to get ready for her trip, and Mr. Wiggles on his way to snack on his leftovers, we went our separate ways.

I took care of my errands, walked back to my car and headed into the office. I needed to pick up some files, and then I was off to my own afternoon appointments. I checked my messages. I'd had a couple of calls from clients and could return those while I was at the office. Also one from my mama. Yeah, I was avoiding her.

CHAPTER EIGHT

It appeared that a three-ring circus had moved into my office since I'd last been there. Was it just yesterday?

I don't usually see animal clients in the office. There's so much I need to know about their environment, and it's usually the pet parents who are the problem — not the pets.

There was a huge Newfoundland, who looked more like a big black bear than a dog, and a Boston Terrier, who had wrapped his leash completely around the hall tree. An adorable but overly excited Bichon Frise had a dog toy and was desperately trying to get someone to play.

Meanwhile, there was an unholy din as first the short-legged brown and black basset hound, and then the young tan and white beagle howled first at each other and then at the rest. In response, a tiny Pekingese lifted his leg and peed on the sundial design oriental carpet in the entryway.

Oh, my.

I made my way through the chaos and to the circular desk in the middle of the room. A frizzy-haired young woman I didn't recognize was on the phone. Her curly dark hair rioted around her face and draped down on a bright yellow and purple smock. She hung up the phone and turned to me, dark eyes blinking furiously.

"Can I help you?"

"What are all these dogs and people doing here?"

"Oh, they're here to see Caro Lamont, the pet therapist."

"I'm her. I'm Caro, the . . ." Sheesh, I was having as much trouble with my own name as I had with April-Mae-June's name. "I'm the pet therapist."

"Great. Then they're here to see you. Who would you like to see first?"

"I don't see patients in the office. Where is Paris?" Paris was our regular receptionist. Before you go there, yes, she does look like that Paris. However, her last name is not the same as the hotel heiress. She normally takes care of all of us in the office complex. There's me, a tax accountant, a real estate agent, and a psychic.

I have to tell you right at that moment I

wished for a little clairvoyance myself. Maybe if I had some special mental powers, I'd be able to figure out what was going on.

"She's gone. I'm LaKeesha, and I'm from the temp agency. People called about their problem pets. That's what you do, right? The schedule says you'd be in the office today at two o'clock, so I told them you'd be in at two and they should just bring their dogs and come on in. Do you have forms they should fill out?"

I tried to hold onto my patience. "No forms. I don't see the animals in my office. I need to see them in their homes."

"Oh." Her bright plum-tone lipsticked mouth made a perfect O.

I turned to look at the room. Besides the fact there were a whole lot of unhappy pet parents, it was a very unstable environment for the dogs. I considered a mass announcement but wasn't sure I could be heard, so I started with the closest dog. The big Newfie. His owner was a tall athletic honey blonde.

"Hi, what's this guy's name?"

"Sassy," she replied. "It's short for Sasquatch."

I smiled at the name. "He's a beautiful guy. I'm afraid there's been a misunderstanding. I don't work with the animals here. If you're interested in my services, I'll need to do an in-home evaluation."

"I thought it was kind of strange, but I didn't know how it worked. And the girl who answered was insistent I just bring Sassy and come in. He's got a problem with destructive behavior, and I'm at my wits end."

Sassy didn't look destructive at the moment. In fact, he was probably the best-behaved pet in the office. I handed her my card. "Call my cell phone, and we'll set up a time for me to come to your house. I'm so sorry for the misunderstanding today. The first visit will be on me."

"Okay, I'll do that." She tugged on his leash, and a very docile Sassy got to his feet and lumbered toward the door with her.

I repeated the talk with each of the clients in the waiting room. Talking a bit with each, I explained how I usually work, and offered the initial consultation free in apology for the mass confusion that had caused them to think they needed to pack up their pooches and come to PAWS.

Once the last doggie/owner duo had left the office, I rounded on LaKeesha.

"Now, what happened to Paris?"

"Dunno. I guess your regular girl quit. I work for a temp agency in the Valley, and they sent me. I'm sorry for the problem with the dogs." She had the grace to look sheepish. "I usually go out on jobs at doctor's offices, and it seemed logical to me for them to come in."

"I can see where you'd think that," I said with a sigh. "Let's see if we can get this place cleaned up."

CHAPTER NINE

I was dead-dog tired. After the day I'd had, I was glad Kitty's sister was in residence next door and had taken over the care of Tobey and Minou. I wanted nothing more than to soak my sore muscles, fix myself a salad and a glass of wine, and maybe sit out on my deck and enjoy the view. Sometimes you just need solitude.

I changed clothes, took Dogbert on a quick around-the-block trek, promised him a longer walk tomorrow, and headed inside to begin my evening of self-indulgence. Just as I slipped my key in the door, I heard a voice calling me from next door.

"Hey there, Caro. Can I talk to you a minute?" She headed across the front lawn as fast as her little legs and four-inch wedgie sandals would take her.

Every time I saw the woman I was struck at the contrast between her and Kitty. Granted both were small-boned, tiny in stature and neither were probably born blondes. But where Kitty's honey blonde highlights had been perfectly salon blended, her sister's flaxen locks had been bleached within an inch of their split ends.

Kitty's petite figure had powered through life all control and focus. April, on the other hand, it seemed had sort of flitted from one thing to the next.

But by far the biggest difference was that Kitty had always been a private person. In all the years we'd shared a fence, she'd never talked about where she was from, what brought her to California, or anything else personal for that matter. April Mae, on the other hand, had no filter. If it popped into her head, it came out her mouth.

Today she wore denim short-shorts that showed off her tanned legs and a leopard-print blouse that criss-crossed her chest and showed off her cleavage. Over the top of it all was a bright polka dot apron that looked like it had been stolen from a fifties sitcom. As she got closer, I could read the saying on the front of it. It said, "Who says beer won't make you smart, it made Bud wiser." Okay, maybe not so *Leave it to Beaver* after all.

"How was your day?" She smiled up at me shading her eyes with her hand.

I sighed inside, hoping for a fast escape,

which was hardly ever the case with April Mae June.

"It was okay," I lied like a rug. It hadn't been an okay day, but it would take more explanation than I was up to. "Any word on Kitty's services?"

"I talked to that good-lookin' detective, and he says they'll be releasing her . . . her body by the end of the week." She sort of hiccupped on the words.

I immediately felt bad for feeling so impatient with her and waited for her to approach.

"Ah, honey, I'm sorry. Is there anything I can do?"

"I hate to ask you, but they want me to pick out some clothes for her and . . ." There was that hiccup again, and as she'd gotten closer I could see her cornflower blue eyes were rimmed in red.

What an awful week the poor woman had been through. She'd driven halfway across the country in a pickup truck with the hope of reuniting with a sister she'd finally found. She arrived only to find her sister was dead. No family. No support.

"You want me to come have a look, sugar?"

I know. I know. I'd been headed directly for a bath and a glass of wine. But she looked so lost.

"If you have time . . ." Her voice trailed off and her blonde curls drooped.

"Of course, I do."

We walked across the lawn and entered the front door. She led the way through the house to Kitty's bedroom suite. It was as elegantly appointed as the woman herself had been.

"I know my sister was a big shot and that she dressed up a lot. I've found pictures of her with all kinds of famous people. Movie stars. People I've only seen in the movies or on TV. So here's what I picked out."

She pointed at a dress she had laid out on the bed.

I hope I didn't gasp out loud. I probably did.

A blindingly bright fuchsia sequined dress lay sprawled across Kitty's elegant Ann Gish damask bedspread.

I was speechless. I wasn't sure when Kitty would have ever worn a dress like that. The only possible explanation was it must have been a Halloween costume.

"Ah, April, ah Mae . . ."

"June," she finished for me.

"Right." I needed to get this name thing straightened out before it drove me loony.

I took a deep breath.

Her hopeful expression almost made me renege, but I owed it to Kitty to keep her from being buried in such a blatant fashion faux pas. I mean, who among us would wear bright fuchsia sequins to a funeral. Even our own. Maybe especially our own.

I took a deep breath again. "Here's the thing. Kitty didn't really wear sequins."

"But she was Hollywood," she insisted. Her squeaky voice got squeakier.

I searched my brain for a reference. Kitty was definitely more Dior and less Versace. Well, shoot. I didn't think designer names were going to help out a whole lot with explaining Kitty's style to her sister.

"Yes, she was Hollywood. But think less Britney Spears and more Catherine Zeta Jones."

She looked puzzled.

"Hollywood, but not flashy Hollywood."

I led her toward Kitty's walk-in closet. Her closet — much like everything in the house — was uber-organized. Suits by color and jacket length. Coordinating shoes in cubicles. There was one area that seemed to be dressier dresses. I quickly looked through the selections.

"Here we go." I held out a deep burgundy dress. This wasn't an off-the-rack frock, but rather must have been custom designed for

Kitty. I'd seen it in one of the pictures in the hallway. It was perfect.

"I don't know."

"Remember the picture of her at the Academy Awards that was in the hall?"

April-Mae-You-Can-Call-Me-June nodded.

"This is what she had on. That night had to be one of the highlights of her life. She looked so happy and so proud of her stars."

April began to tear up.

"I'll bet she kept the dress because it was a big moment. And this would be a wonderful way to celebrate her life and her accomplishments." I could see she was weakening on the sequins.

She sniffed but nodded in agreement.

"Okay then." I picked up matching shoes and brought them and the dress out of the closet. I needed to keep her moving before she changed her mind. "Let's put them in a garment bag."

I moved out of the bedroom and down the hallway, hoping she'd follow.

I stopped in front of the picture of Kitty at the Academy Awards. "Do you want to send this picture to the funeral home with the dress, so they can make sure her hair and everything is right?"

I didn't know if that was an acceptable

thing or not, but keeping April on task seemed the important goal at the moment.

I turned back to see if she was following, and that's when my better judgment and self-survival slipped away.

Big old tears had dragged rivers of mascara down her cheeks, and she looked so gosh-darn bedraggled that I couldn't help myself.

"Do you want to come over for dinner?" I heard myself offering.

"Oh, that would be super!" Her face brightened, and she rubbed at her cheeks. "Just let me . . ."

"Good golly!" she suddenly shrieked.

"What?"

"Would you look at me?" We'd passed the big art deco mirror that hung on the wall between the hall and the living room, and she'd caught sight of herself. "Lordy. I look like I was drug through a knot-hole backwards."

I had to agree she did look a little the worse for wear, but hey, who wouldn't with what she'd been through.

"Tell you what." I patted her arm. "You take a few minutes to freshen up, and I'll go get our food started. You come on over whenever you're ready."

"Okie dokie, I'll be there in two shakes of

a lamb's tail." She shook her hips and giggled at herself.

Oh, my. I headed back across the lawn to my house. Well, the prospect of dinner had certainly cheered her up, but what had I gotten myself into?

My evening of relaxation and pampering had turned into entertaining April — ah Mae — ah.

Well, one thing for sure. This evening wasn't going to be a total waste. I was determined to get straight what the heck I was supposed to call the woman.

CHAPTER TEN

When April-Mae-You-Can-Call-Me-June arrived, she appeared to be in better shape and better spirits. She'd traded her short shorts for a sundress, and though she still looked like a Cover Girl commercial gone awry, she'd cleaned up the runny zombie eye make-up.

"I didn't know what we were having, but I brought this." She held a wine bottle aloft.

I took it from her and glanced at the label. "Very nice. I'll put it in the chiller."

"I usually drink beer. A Coors if I'm bein' real fancy. But Sissy didn't seem to have any beer."

No, I'll bet she didn't. I wondered when she'd decided to call Kitty "Sissy."

"Let's eat out on the patio, if you don't mind."

"Sounds like fun."

I'd set up placemats and matching dishes for the occasion. Pretty chic for me. My mama would be proud. I'd thrown together a salmon salad with toasted almonds and added homemade bruschetta with tomato and basil I'd made from some bread I'd picked up at the Laguna Beach Farmers Market.

"This looks great."

We didn't talk for a little while as we dug in. Both of us had apparently worked up an appetite.

I looked across the table at my dinner companion and considered my approach. I was determined to get this name thing settled. I decided on direct.

"Is April Mae your given name?" I asked.

"No." She shook blonde curls.

"It's not? Then June is your given name?"

"No again." She giggled.

"Okay, sugar, help me out here. I'm trying to figure out what I should call you."

"Well, as Harriet Hickenhopper, one of my foster mamas, used to say, 'Call me anything you want 'cept don't call me late to supper.' " She snickered at her own joke. "She was one of the good ones."

This wasn't really helping me. I tried a different tack.

"What does your family in Eminence, Missouri call you?"

"Sissy. But they call every female relative Sissy."

All right, this was getting ridiculous. I would get a straight answer if it took all night.

"What name is on your driver's license?"

"April Mae Wooben. The last foster family I was with actually adopted me, and so I've kept their last name all these years."

"And most people in Eminence call you April Mae?"

"No, hardly anybody does. But you can if you want to. It is my name, after all."

She took a breath, and I managed to interject. "Explain."

"You see, my name was such a joke when I was a little kid that everyone called me April Mae June, and pretty soon everyone was just callin' me June, and you know how it is. It stuck. So most everyone back home calls me June."

We sat in silence for a while as April Mae June thought about her childhood. At least I imagined she did. During the silence, I thought about how I wasn't any closer to knowing what the heck I should call her.

"But I think June is a better California name, more sophisticated like. So I'm gonna go by that out here. What do you think? Or maybe I should come up with a whole other name, like Kitty did. I like the animal theme. Maybe I'll call myself Chickie. Like Chickie Monkey. Are they real animals, Chickie Monkeys? I'm not sure. Sounds cute though, doesn't it. Did you ever wish for a different name?"

What I wished for was a way I could go back in time and not have invited her for dinner.

"No, I'm kind of okay with my name." Though I did take back my maiden name when I divorced my cheating ex-husband, Geoffrey Carlise. Still, I wasn't going to cloud this already murky conversation by sharing that information.

"Do you think there are real Chickie Monkeys?"

"No, I think it's an expression like 'cheeky monkey.' I don't think it's actually a breed of monkey."

"Oh well, maybe I'll stick with June then."

"Sorry?" I was sorry. Very sorry I'd ever thought this would be simple, and very sorry I'd thought it was a good topic for dinner conversation. I needed an escape.

"I'm going to get a corkscrew and pour some of the wine you brought for us. I'll be right back." I stood.

"Oh, it's not a twist off kinda bottle, huh?"

"No, it's not." I left April-Mae-June-

Chickie-Monkey-Wooben on the patio and sprinted to the refuge of my kitchen. I wondered how long I could stay away before she'd come looking for me. I located a corkscrew, leaned against the counter and enjoyed the quiet. I could see the patio and my guest from the kitchen.

Feeling uncharitable for my un-hostess-like thoughts, I knew I couldn't leave her out there. My mama was one tough cookie, but she had raised us to know what our duty was when we had company.

I opened the wine, let it breath, picked up a couple of wine glasses and headed back outside.

"You're so lucky." April Mae looked up.

Yes, that's right. *April Mae.* Despite all the discussion and her preference to be called June while in California. She looked like an April Mae, not a June, and that's what I would call her.

"Lucky? How so?" She was right, I was extremely lucky. I was happy and healthy. I lived in a gorgeous community. Made a living doing something I loved.

"You have a family who loves you, and you know even if you fight with them they're always there for you." She was right again. My family made me crazy, but I loved them, and I knew they loved me. We had each other's backs.

Wait a doggone minute.

How did April Mae know anything about my family? I'd never shared anything about my background. I felt the hairs on the back of my neck tingle. I had a bad feeling about this.

"April Mae, how do you know about my family?"

"You can call me —"

"Stop it. I'm calling you April Mae. I've decided." I carefully set my wine down on the table. "How do you know about fighting with my family?"

"Oh, honey, I apologize. I meant to tell you earlier that your cousin stopped by."

"My cousin?"

"Yep, your cousin, Melinda. She needed to get into your house, and her key didn't work. I was outside getting some stuff outta the truck. Your cousin wondered if I happened to have a key, and I looked through Kitty's keys, and she had one labeled with your name. I tell you that sister of mine was one organized woman. No wonder she was so successful as a businesswoman."

I heard her pattering on, but I'd stopped listening.

"That wretch!" I exploded.

"Well, that's an awful thing to say about

85

someone. Especially someone who's dead and can't defend themselves. I thought you were Kitty's friend."

"Not your sister, my cousin."

I pushed back from the table and hurried to my bedroom. I'd been careless. I'd left the brooch pinned to the dress I'd worn the night of the Paw Prints exhibition.

I'd even made it easy for her. I'd made sure there was a picture of me in the dress in the newspaper column covering the event. Mel's pig-headed but not stupid, and so she'd waltzed into my house, located the dress, and took the pin.

I'd left the classy Kate Spade dress on the end, meaning to find a hiding place for the brooch and to drop the dress off at the cleaners. It still sported the cat and dog hair from the event. It no longer sported the brooch.

"Argghhh!"

"What's wrong, sweetie?" April had followed me. "Are you okay?"

I explained about the brooch.

"Oh, no. I am so sorry. Your cousin seemed so nice."

"Well she's not. She's a . . . a . . . thief. A brooch-taker."

"Oh, I am so sorry. I didn't know. What have I done?" The sprite wrung her hands in distress.

I realized I'd scared the poor woman. She wasn't privy to the fact that the brooch stealing was an on-going thing.

"Don't worry," I tossed the dress on the bed. "I'll figure out a way to get it back."

April Mae came to stand by my side. "And I'll help you."

CHAPTER ELEVEN

The media continued to speculate about Kitty's death. I turned on my television the next morning to an announcement about Kitty's funeral and discussion of the incident.

"According to a Laguna Beach official who had been briefed by the police, the investigation team is working on a theory of shots fired from another vehicle into Bardot's BMW which was traveling north here on Pacific Coast Highway." A reporter stood near where Kitty's car had crashed. I felt a return of the same sick feeling I'd felt that night.

I sliced a mango and perched on the arm of the sofa. So, we were finally speculating about a shooter. Dogbert parked himself beside me, not sure what was on my plate. I didn't feed him table scraps. Ever. But Dogbert was at heart an optimist. He was sure my resolve could waver at any moment, and, to tell you the truth, it was hard to resist his hopeful puppy-dog eyes.

"What about theories circulating around a sniper shooting?" asked the anchor.

"Oh, please. Not a sniper," I barked at the reporter, waving my knife at the screen. Laguna Beach was not exactly a high crime area. We had the occasional party that got out of hand, the infrequent domestic dispute, tons of illegal parking. Maybe drive-by moonings, but not drive-by shootings.

All we needed was the mass hysteria of a community waiting for more shots to ring out.

"At this point," said the reporter on the scene, "the investigation is wide-open. Police aren't sure if this was random, if Bardot was targeted, and if she was the intended target, what the motive could have been. They've not ruled anything out."

The TV shot switched back to the studio, and the tone turned somber as the reporter noted, "Services for Kitty Bardot will be this Friday at 10:00 AM. She was a popular publicist to a number of Hollywood's hottest stars, and we expect many of her clients will be in attendance."

"And she won't be wearing pink sequins," I finished for them.

Dogbert tipped his doggie head in question.

"Well, she won't," I told him.

I really, really did not want to go to this funeral, but when April Mae had asked, well, what could I say?

The services were to be held at the Westwood Village Memorial Park and Mortuary, a nonpareil LA cemetery and the final resting place of many of Hollywood's brightest stars. And, for that matter, many of its tragic women. Marilyn Monroe, Natalie Wood, and Dorothy Stratten, to name a few.

Also, music legends like Roy Orbison and Frank Zappa and Keith Richards. No wait, that's not right, Keith Richards isn't dead. He just looks dead.

In any case, according to April Mae, Kitty had detailed the exact arrangements in her will. There was to be a memorial service open to friends but the actual interment private. According to the gossips, she was to be buried near Farrah Fawcett. Who knew if it was true or not. There was lots of gossip making the rounds, and with each round, like one of Grandpa Montgomery's fish stories, the details grew.

We found the place easily, but parking was packed. I looked up at the open A-frame chapel. A natural stone wall rose at the front, and surrounding windows afforded a beautiful view of the grounds. The place was mostly filled when we arrived, but Paul Kantor, Kitty's attorney, motioned us forward to some chairs near the front where he'd saved two seats. A little too close to Kitty's casket for my taste.

I'd met Kantor before as he was also Diana's attorney. He was a blend-into-the-background sort of guy. Average height, average looks. Very formal manners.

All eyes were on us as we made our way to the front. I'd worn a simple black silk Dolce and Gabbana dress; April Mae wore a sundress. I'd loaned her a silver and black Oscar de la Renta scarf, which thankfully covered most of the peek-a-boo polyester dress.

Don't get me wrong, it wasn't so much that I cared what the rich and famous thought of her discount store garb. But you couldn't be around April Mae for long without feeling protective of her, and I didn't want to see her become the object of ridicule. It was nobody's dang business what Kitty's sister's circumstances were.

I tried not to stare at the many famous faces who glanced up as we passed. I'd known Kitty had this other life where she mingled with big stars, attended premiers, and brokered promotional deals. But to me, Kitty had always just been a friendly neighbor and fellow pet lover.

Kantor stood until we were seated. April Mae and I settled in our chairs.

The service was short and sweet. The official wasted no time. I couldn't tell whether he was a minister or not. In the movie community sometimes it's hard to tell if a person is really a minister or just plays one. Whoever he was, he did a very nice reading of Kitty's obituary, detailing of her accomplishments, and then the service closed with a musical tribute by several of her clients from the music business who sang together on a medley of "Amazing Grace." I don't exactly follow the music scene, but I did know the good-looking trio leading the song had won a Grammy last year. It was moving.

By the time the song was over, April Mae was in full sob mode. I searched my purse for tissues and handed several to her. On the one hand, I didn't blame her, and, heck, Kitty deserved someone shedding tears over her. On the other hand, I remembered her emotional faint the first day I'd met her, and I sincerely hoped she could gain control before we had to pick her up off the shiny marble floor.

The attorney looked at me with an expression that said "help."

"Oh shoot, sugar." I put my arm around her. "Just cry it out."

She leaned into me and wailed.

Kitty would have been appalled. My mama would have been horrified.

You know what? I didn't give a flying fruitcake what kind of scene April caused.

The attorney looked at me again. This time with an expression that said, "Not the kind of help I was looking for."

April finally stopped. Her waterworks had soaked my shoulder and destroyed her makeup, but she was under control. I handed her another wad of tissues.

"Sorry," she whispered with a small snuffle.

It was too late to be quiet now.

As we got up to leave, I could see most of the celebrities had taken off. I didn't blame them. Though the press hadn't been allowed in the service, they'd waited right outside, microphones in hand, ready to pounce.

I nodded to Franklin Chesney, Kitty's partner in the PR firm, who was in the row just behind us. I'd worked with him and his dogs, an elderly pair of Corgis. I knew he'd recently lost the two, within weeks of each other. The dogs had been seventeen, which is old for the breed. He'd been a good dog daddy to the elderly pair, and I knew he had to be missing them.

Franklin was impeccably dressed, as always. His pin-striped suit was custom-tailored for his tall, thin frame. His bald head shone from the light of the overhead chandelier. He looked exhausted, his eyes red-rimmed and tired. He and Kitty had seemed close, and I imagined that in addition to grieving the loss of a business partner and good friend, he was also scrambling to deal with clients who now wondered what was going to happen to them.

I recognized only a few others. A few of the locals. Some members of the Laguna Beach art community. Kitty had been a very active part of that crowd. Grey would know most of them. The crowd seemed to be mostly Hollywood.

While I'm sure most were there to pay their respects, and they may have thought highly of Kitty Bardot, it seemed April Mae was the only one in the house who showed any real emotion.

As I turned to pick up my bag, I noticed Tonya Miles, a friend of Kitty's, who I'd often seen at her home. It had seemed an odd combination to me. Kitty was all business. Tonya was all face-lifts and flash.

As was her hallmark, Tonya's nails were perfection, her bleached blonde hair was sprayed within an inch of its life, and her outfit was couture. Her perfect black frock was accented by a Hermes scarf with a Pegasus pattern. I thought the winged horse design was a year or two old, but the da Vinci-like drawing was a classic. Tonya was the ex-wife of Cy Miles, one of the major Hollywood producers. His movies made millions, and it looked like he needed to keep the box office hits coming to keep his ex in style. She dabbed at the corner of one eye with the scarf. The horse's tush, I think, to be exact.

Across the aisle I also noticed the artist Sam and I had sat by at the art event the night Kitty had died.

Clive. I remembered his name because my daddy once had a horse trainer named Clive, who I'd kind of had a crush on as a teenager. He'd been a great trainer and very good-looking, which he used to his advantage with all the Montgomery girl cousins.

This Clive was a handsome guy, too. At least when his eyes and nose weren't all red. I remembered at the Montage event Sam had asked him about allergies. You had to question the sanity of attending an animal artist event when you're allergic to cats. Sheesh. Must have been really important to see and be seen.

His square jaw had strategic fashionable stubble, dark brooding brows above unnaturally aqua blue eyes, longish dark hair. He wasn't tall but still drew your gaze.

He'd collected a small crowd around him, mostly female. He seemed to be holding forth on how close he and Kitty had been and how devastated he was by the loss of his dear friend.

I didn't know how Kitty had done it. At least all I dealt with was doggie drama and the like. When you dealt with people with this kind of star power, it was always all about them.

"Before you leave, I'd like to have a moment of your time." Paul Kantor, the attorney, spoke to April Mae. "The facility has offered the use of their private consultation room."

"I can wait outside or in the car."

She clutched my arm. "No." April Mae shook her head and nodded toward me. "I want Caro to come with me."

"Is that okay?" I asked, a bit unsure of proper after-the-funeral etiquette with a lawyer.

Kantor nodded assent and indicated a

hallway. People still filed out the back of the room. We slipped down the hall and into a well-appointed conference room with deep soft carpet. April and I sat down and Kantor seated himself across the table.

"Ms. Wooben." He tented his hands and leaned in. "As I told you when we talked on the phone, Ms. Bardot left the majority of her estate to you. Her will, which is three years old, is worded, 'To my sister, if found.' "

"That's so sweet." April Mae's hands went to her cheeks. "Caro, wasn't that sweet?"

I nodded. Sweet wasn't the word for it. I was blown away. Kitty had never even met her sister, and her Laguna Beach property alone was worth millions.

"Now, I have every reason to believe from the correspondence you've provided to me that Ms. Bardot believed you were her sister. I will need to, of course, verify through legal means that is indeed the case."

"What does that mean?" April's head swiveled between the attorney and me and back to him.

"It means I'll go through your adoption records, foster care records, and Ms. Bardot's."

"Oh."

"As the executor, I have filed the will with

the court, and, of course, a copy will be provided to all the beneficiaries."

"O-okay." Bless her heart, the poor thing looked shell-shocked.

I wondered who the other beneficiaries were, but April Mae didn't ask and it wasn't my place. Darn it all.

"In the meantime, the estate will continue to pay Ms. Bardot's bills," Mr. Kantor continued. "And you may stay at the house, if you choose. Or you may return to your home. This process can take a few months."

"I'm not going anywhere until they find out who killed my sister." April Mae straightened in her chair. "Someone shot Sissy. Took her life. And because of them, I never got to know her. The least I can do is hang in here and see them brought to justice." Her voice cracked with the declaration.

"That's fine," he said.

I wondered if he were really listening.

"You let me know if you change your mind. We can see about putting the house on the market and liquidating the rest of her assets." Kantor might as well have been speaking Sam's native Greek for all April Mae understood of what he'd said.

"Okey dokey," she answered, bobbing her head. "Are we done? Caro, you've got to feed me. I'm just plain starving. I didn't eat a thing this morning, I was so wound up about the funeral, and now I'm feeling puny."

"No problem, sugar. We'll get you something."

The lawyer handed April his business card and stood. "You can call me if you have questions."

"Thank you." She gave him a big bear hug.

Now the attorney looked shell-shocked.

The place had cleared out, and as we stepped outside it looked like the press had moved on. Thank God.

I feared April Mae would fall in the five-inch high-heeled sandals she'd chosen to wear, but she was intent on lunch and quickly teetered her way across the parking lot to my car.

I wondered where to take her. I had a sudden thought and turned the car to Riccio's.

Dino Riccio, Diana's current beau was a good friend and his restaurant would be perfect. I knew his staff would put us in an area where we wouldn't be bothered and take good care of us.

It wasn't far to the restaurant. Riccio's was decorated with warm Tuscany tones and old-world charm. Pictures of Dino's ancestors dotted the walls. He wasn't there, but the maitre d' recognized me from other visits, and I asked if we could have a quiet corner. It was lunchtime, so the place was busy, but he put us in an alcove near the back that was semi-private.

I picked a light California wine, and the waiter poured a glass for each of us while we looked over the menu.

Once we'd ordered, I lifted my wine glass in salute. "To Kitty."

April Mae lifted hers and smiled. "To Kitty. I wish I'd gotten a chance to know her."

We sat in silence for a little while, each of us lost in our own thoughts.

April Mae eventually broke the silence. "Well, though I didn't get to know my sister, I've had the chance to get to know you and some of her other neighbors. It sounds like she was a real nice lady." April Mae leaned back in her chair.

"She was. I didn't know her well, but we've always been cordial over the years." I'd genuinely liked Kitty Bardot.

"On the TV they said there was some talk about a sniper. Do you think that's a possibility?"

"I suppose it could be. I'm sure the police are looking into every possibility." I felt my eye twitch as I remembered my promise to Malone that I would mind my own business.

"I haven't heard anything from them at all." April shook her blonde curls. "Here's what I do know. I know somebody killed my sister, and they need to pay." She scooted to the edge of her seat.

"The police will find out who did it," I said firmly. "You know, sometimes they're tracking down leads, but you may not hear anything while the investigation is going on." I leaned forward and looked her in the eye. April Mae didn't need to know I'd learned this the hard way.

"Let's go over the suspects." She ignored me completely. "There's the road rage theory. But I don't think the police think it was road rage. Then there's the random shooter. Just some fool with a gun shootin' for the fun of it. I don't know why somebody would do that. If not road rage or a shooter, it has to be somebody who knew my sister and had something against her. Who would that be?"

"April Mae, hon, I don't know who that would be. There's no one I can think of that benefited from Kitty's death."

No one except for the little pixie across the table from me. And while I thought

April Mae was a flake, I didn't think she was a cold-blooded killer.

"Hmmm." She tapped her wine glass with a candy pink fingernail while she thought.

"Did Kitty have any other family?" I'd wondered if there'd been just the sisters. *Great, now she'd sucked me in.*

"None I know of. There was just us two. I don't know if she tried to find our parents or not over the years, but the private detective who contacted me said he didn't know anything about them."

The waiter arrived with our food and refilled our wine glasses. As always at Dino's, the food smelled delicious, and I was sure it would taste just as good. We both dug in.

"Speakin' of family, Caro." Her eyes narrowed. "I found out where that sneaky cousin of yours is keeping your brooch." April Mae had taken it very personal that Mel had used her to get into my house.

"You did? Where is it?" My head snapped up, melted mozzarella halfway to my mouth. I'd thought long and hard about what Mel might do now that she had Grandma Tillie's brooch again.

"Your cousin, Melinda, has it right in plain sight in a locked display case in her store. I went in there to get some botanical kitty cat shampoo for Tobey and Minou, and I saw it."

Ah, that sounded like Mel. Hidden in plain sight where it was always under her watchful eyes. But, then again, where she hoped someone would see it and tell me.

And she was right, someone had.

"Wow." I put my fork down, my appetite gone. I considered the possibilities. Maybe a nighttime foray? If she had an alarm system, getting into the store could present a problem. "This could be a challenge."

"Not so much." April Mae smiled an impish grin.

"How so?" I tore off a piece of bread absently and reached for the dipping oil.

April Mae looked around for listeners and leaned forward. "Well, between me and you, I had a few problems as a teenager growing up in different foster families. One of the families I was placed with was a mom and dad who were shoplifters. And, I tell you, they were good at what they did. They taught us kids how to steal things, mostly because no one pays any attention to the kids."

"Ah, sugar, that's awful."

"It wasn't for very long. I was only ten, and I told my family counselor about it. They got arrested, and I got transferred to a new family, but not before I'd picked up a few tricks."

Oh, my. The pixie was a shoplifter.

"If you can figure out a way to distract your cousin, I can get the brooch." She snapped her fingers in the air. "Piece of cake."

I felt bad. I really did. I mean encouraging larceny.

But desperate times call for desperate measures, and I had to get my Grandma Tillie's brooch back.

I knew exactly how to distract Mel. All I needed to do was waltz into the store, and all eyes would be on me.

Caro Lamont in the Bow Wow Boutique?

No one would be looking anywhere else. It could work.

CHAPTER TWELVE

Thank goodness more exciting events were happening in the news, and media attention had waned on covering Kitty's death. It was a great day when I came home, and all the news vans were gone from across the street.

I had every intention of staying out of Detective Malone's investigation. I'd taken a mind-my-own-business vow. The police had this one. No innocent person was sitting in jail, accused of a crime she hadn't committed. Malone and his crew were actively tracking down Kitty's killer.

Too bad April Mae hadn't taken the same vow. Once she'd gotten word from the attorney that she was cleared to stay at Kitty's and that she was the primary beneficiary, the woman was on a mission.

Each day she had an update for me.

Today I was stopping by Diana's to check in with Bella as promised, and then meeting my pal, Walt, for coffee. I'd asked April Mae if she'd like to go along partly to try to keep her out of trouble and partly because I wanted Walt to meet her. It was impossible to just describe her.

The guard checked us through the entry to Ruby Point, and from the awestruck look on April Mae's face you would have thought we were entering Disneyland.

As I parked in Diana's flower-lined driveway, and as we got out of the car, April Mae's sharp intake of breath made me remember the first time I'd seen the place.

"This is where Diana Knight lives?" she whispered.

Graceful and elegant, the front of the mansion was lush with flower beds filled with roses and other blooms.

I couldn't ever walk past Diana's flowers without a flashback to a few months earlier. The police had dug up her flowers looking for a murder weapon. In fact, Diana was still plenty steamed about the roses. But that's a story for another time, and one Diana loves to tell.

We rang the doorbell, and Bella answered. The barking in the background told me things were business as usual at Diana's.

"Come in, *damas.*" The dark-haired Bella ushered us inside.

"How is it going, Bella?" I asked over the din.

"Not so bad, Caro." Her musical Spanish lilt complemented her warm smile. "My nephew, he comes by and helps me take the dogs to walk. Like you say, they are better behaved when they get some exercise."

I was a big proponent of making sure pets get plenty of exercise, and Diana was one of the few of my clients who always made sure her animals were exercised.

In the pampered world of Bark Mitzvahs, Mommy and Me doggie yoga, pet massage, paw soaks and peticures, and even pet chauffeurs to shuttle dogs and cats to their appointments, it was not a message always well received. Bella had heard my lecture before and supported the idea.

"This is my neighbor, April Mae." I introduced the pixie who was busy taking in the splendor of the mansion's foyer.

Elegant styling, high-end marble, and classic old world furnishings contrasted with April Mae's fashion statement created sort of a through-the-looking-glass sensation. Her outfit of the day was a skin-tight pink and white plaid cami-top and white jeans. She'd accessorized with a large pink hair bow that completely dwarfed her tiny form. And shiny silver vinyl sandals.

Bella didn't even blink.

"Nice to meet you." She extended her hand to April Mae. "I am so sorry for your loss."

"Thank you." April teared up at the kindness, and instead of accepting Bella's hand, she hugged her.

All I could figure was they must do a ton of hugging in Eminence, Missouri.

Bella, bless her heart, hugged April Mae back and patted her shoulder.

"Is there anything you need? Anything we can help with?" I asked Bella. The noise had quieted, and Mr. Wiggles had scampered into the entry to have his belly scratched. Next came Barbary, Diana's one-eyed basset hound, who also wanted some attention. April Mae and I obliged.

"I think we are good." Bella reached down and patted the dogs. "For a zoo," she added with a smile. "You know Miss Diana she got a second goat? *La cabra,* a girl goat."

"No, I didn't know." I laughed. "What's the deal with her?"

"She is from the animal rescue. Her name is Henny, and she has really big eyes." Bella held her fingers like goggles. "*Muy grandes.* Very big."

"Can we see her?" April Mae was, of

course, thrilled with the idea of a big-eyed goat.

"She seemed to be not well. Falling down sometimes. I called Dr. Daniel, the animal doctor. He took her for a look. I hope that was the right thing to do."

"Exactly what I would have done," I assured her. "Let me know what Dr. Daniel says and if you need any help getting Henny picked up."

"He said he will look her over and report."

"All right then, we won't keep you." I tugged on April Mae's arm. "You call if you need anything."

Bella thanked us and held the pooches so they wouldn't try to follow us out the door.

Just as we were about to get back in the car, I heard angry voices and a yelp from beyond the mountain lilac hedge that separated Diana's yard from her neighbors'.

I pushed through the hedge. A big beefy man in a suit spanked a little black-and-tan Yorkie with a newspaper. A dark-haired delicate looking woman wrapped in a too-large sweater begged him to stop, her voice high-pitched and yippy.

"Stop it, you're hurting her. Bitty didn't mean to piddle in your shoes. She had to go, and you frightened her." The woman tried without success to stop the assault on the dog, but the guy brushed her off as if she were a gnat.

"That little rat has got to be taught she can't pee anywhere she pleases. I work damn hard for the things we have, and you can't control her. Those loafers were Gucci." His voice boomed, making both the woman and the dog cower.

Enough.

I saw red. I marched up to Bluto, yanked the newspaper from his hand, and boxed his ears with it.

"What the Sam Hill do you think you're doin'?" I punctuated my question with another smack. My red-headed temperament comes out a bit stronger when I'm upset, and I was plenty upset. "Hittin' a dog is no way to train it."

"How does this feel?" I smacked him upside the head one more time for good measure. "Kinda makes you want to pee in your penny loafers, doesn't it?"

The look on He-Man's face was priceless. His meaty cheeks were stretched tight by his stunned expression, his eyebrows frozen like exclamation points. He looked like one of those cartoon characters just before steam shoots out the top of their head.

"I don't know who you think you are coming onto my property and assaulting me," he shouted. "But you can march your pretty little ass right back where you came from and mind your own business." His face glowed with fury.

"Or I'll call the police," he added for good measure.

"Oh, yeah, let's do that." I pulled out my cell phone. Out of the corner of my eyes, I saw the woman reach for the dog. "Let's make sure we ask for Sgt. Peterson who's in charge of animal cruelty."

I could see a flicker of doubt in his eyes. I had him. He was unsure. Then like most cornered beasts, he went on the attack.

He stepped forward into my space, but I refused to give any ground. "You've made your point. Now, back off."

He-man turned on his heel and headed toward a bright yellow Corvette parked in the driveway, climbed in, and squealed his tires down the street.

"Thanks." The woman's voice was so low I could barely hear her. Without ever making eye contact, she slipped inside the house, the door shutting with a click.

Adrenalin still pumping, I pounded on the door. Anyone who would pick on a little dog probably had no hesitation about smacking around the woman in his life. I had to know if she was okay.

After several minutes of ringing the bell and pounding on the door, it was clear to me she was not going to answer. I sighed and glanced at the newspaper still clutched in my hand.

I searched through my handbag and pulled out a PAWS business card and a pen. "If you need help, please call me," I scrawled on it and tucked it inside the paper. I prayed she would know I meant help, not just for the dog, but for her.

I turned to go and ran smack into April Mae, who'd followed.

"You were awesome!" April Mae squealed as I pushed back through the hedge to my car. She followed, jumping up and down, her pink bow about to bounce off her head.

I couldn't talk, I was still so mad.

"Get in the car," I finally managed to say.

Leaving Diana's driveway, I headed to the Ruby Point exit but drove slowly past the house next door. I didn't know who Diana's new neighbors were, but I would find out. I was still worried about the woman and the little dog as I drove out and back to downtown Laguna. You work with enough people and pets, and it becomes pretty easy to spot a bully.

Walt Cambrian is not only my pal, he'd

been my stepfather's college roommate and was a long-time Montgomery family friend. The Koffee Klatch was packed, but Walt had already snagged an outside table. He was busy snapping pictures. Birds, tourists, bad drivers. Anyone within range of his lens was a potential target.

"Walt, this is April Mae Wooben, Kitty Bardot's sister. April Mae, this is Walt Cambrian. The grumpy one is Walt, the friendly one there is Millie." I patted Walt's Norwich Terrier on the head and gave her a snuggle.

"I'll grab our drinks. What would you like?"

April Mae thought for a moment. "A café mocha with extra whipped cream."

Of course. Any sprinkles or just plain?

By the time I got back with my usual hazelnut latte and April's frothy drink, she was regaling Walt with story of how I'd single-handedly taken on the bad guy next door to Diana Knight with only a folded newspaper as a weapon.

"You shoulda seen it, Walt. Caro was awesome!"

I set the drinks down and slipped into the folding chair.

"How've you been?" I patted Walt's knee, eager to change the subject.

"No complaints." His gravelly voice still

held a chuckle.

Well, I knew that wasn't true. Walt always had a complaint. If the sky was blue, he'd complain we needed rain. If it were raining, he worried about flooding.

"Say Walt, you don't know of anyone looking for a great employee, do you?" When I'd picked up our drinks I'd asked Verdi if she'd had any luck finding something to replace her soon-to-end full-time job.

"Don't know of anything off the top of my head. Why do you ask?"

I explained about Verdi, and Walt said he would be on the lookout for any openings.

"Thanks, Walt." I sipped my latte. "What's the buzz around town?" If anyone knew the scoop around town, it would be him.

"There's talk the police have video of the shooter from the security camera outside of Time Keepers. Apparently they'd had some vandalism and had security cameras installed. They think that's where the shots came from."

"Walt, stop. Not about that." I could understand why he'd thought we'd be interested, but I truly had been trying to keep my nose out of Malone's investigation. Also trying to *not* encourage the little hugging pixie to hunt for Kitty's killer.

"What's Time Keepers?" April Mae asked.

"Time Keepers is a watch shop on Pacific Coast Highway near where Kitty's car crashed," Walt explained.

"There hasn't been anything on the news about video." Okay, I couldn't help myself. This wasn't investigating. I wasn't asking anyone any questions. Surely a girl could be excused a bit of simple curiosity.

And Walt was too good of a source to pass up. He was not only the grumpy-old-guy blogger, he was the best eavesdropper I knew.

"Not yet, but you can't keep a secret around here. I heard at the Art Museum Ms. Bardot'd had an argument with Philippe Arman the day before she died."

"Who is Philippe Arman?" April Mae pounced on the tidbit of gossip right away.

"He owns an art gallery up on North Coast Highway," Walt explained.

"I think his was the gallery that'd been showing the cats', Tobey and Minou's, paintings," I said.

I was sure Walt snorted, but when I looked at him, his face was expressionless.

April Mae had missed it; she was focused on the argument between her sister and the gallery owner.

She was determined to question Philippe Arman. I'd tried to explain it would be best to share the info with Detective Malone and let him follow-up, but she was not to be deterred.

We left Walt sipping coffee, taking pictures and feeding Millie dog treats, and headed back to my car.

CHAPTER THIRTEEN

"I understand if you don't want to be involved, Caro." She carefully buckled her seatbelt. "And if you want, you can just take me home, and I'll go by myself."

Well, heck no. I wasn't going to let her do that.

"Would you at least call Malone and give him the information." I owed the detective at least a minimum of effort before I got in over my head.

She agreed and made the call as we headed north on PCH to the Arman Gallery. She got Malone's voicemail and left a message. I was familiar with the difficulty in reaching Malone live. I'd been down that road before.

"When we question this guy do you want to be the bad cop or the good cop?" April asked, serious as a heart attack.

"What?" I turned to look at her. How had this morphed so quickly? "April Mae, hon,

I think it would be better if we didn't really question the gallery owner. We might have better luck with him if we just kind of act like customers and see if we can get him to talk about Kitty. Sometimes it's more likely a person will share information when they're off guard."

"Oh, I get it. Kind of like we're under-cover, right."

I could hear Malone's lecture in my head.

"I don't see a badge, Ms. Lamont. When did you join the Laguna Beach Police Department?"

But I couldn't let April Mae go it alone.

"Yes, kind of like we're undercover." It would be a miracle if we got through this without a leave-this-to-the-professionals speech from Malone.

"So, we should pretend we're rich ladies, and we're looking for pictures?"

"Art," I clarified. I didn't point out that one of us was a rich lady, or about to be anyway, and the other was just a fairly well-off lady with a trust fund and a decent animal therapy practice that kept her in Manolo Blahniks.

April Mae would eventually come to understand her inheritance was not only a helluva lot of money, it was a life-changing amount of money.

"Gotcha. We're in the market for some art." She was enjoying this way too much.

"That's the general idea. We go in, we look at the art, then we ask some questions, and see if we can steer the conversation to Kitty."

"Right." She straightened her shoulders and then her bow.

"Hopefully we can get a read on how the man felt about your sister. Maybe he'll even mention having talked with her the day before she died."

"Got it."

We'd found a parking spot near the Arman Gallery, which in Laguna Beach is a miracle in itself. Parking, even in the fall — outside of tourist season — is at a premium.

The first thing you noticed about Philippe Arman was his hair. A full head of wavy silver locks, set off by an all-over tan. A tan so even it could not have come from time on Main Beach.

"Hello, ladies." He greeted us the minute we walked into the gallery. The walls surrounding us were adorned with colorful seascapes and intricate sea shells in singular portrait style.

"Hi, we're rich and we're looking for pictures," April Mae spoke up. She looked at me for confirmation, and my face must have registered my dismay. Maybe I should have covered more clearly exactly what we'd say. "Art, really," she corrected and flapped her eyelashes at him.

"What type of art did you have in mind?" He turned to me. I'm sure we presented an interesting pair. She, the curly-headed blonde sprite with a bow on top. Me, the tall red-haired, jean-clad Texas girl.

I towered over April Mae. And I'd worn flats.

"I like abstracts," I offered quickly.

"Ah, if you'll come with me." He moved toward a doorway into another room and motioned for us to follow.

This room didn't contain seascapes which, don't get me wrong, I enjoy. But unlike the first area, this section was populated with various groupings of paintings. There were several I liked, several I didn't, some I didn't get at all, and still others where I could appreciate the technique but found disturbing. But then art, especially abstract art, is very subjective. Which is actually what I find fascinating about it.

I was drawn to a painting by an artist, Thea Hurd. I wasn't terribly educated about art, but I found the stories told by the various pieces interesting.

"This is pretty." April pointed to a swirling pastel. "But I don't know if it will go with my couch."

I believe old Philippe actually shuddered at the statement.

April had broken the cardinal rule in the art world. Art is not an accessory for your home. It's art.

But before he could give April the dressing down reserved for blatant violators, a little fur ball made a preemptive strike. A small dog bed was nestled in one corner, and a handsome little Shih Tzu jumped from the bed and scampered toward April Mae.

In typical April Mae style, she leaned down with a friendly hand and the two became instant pals. "Oh my goodness," she exclaimed. "Is he yours?"

She smiled up at Philippe, and I swear all the air went out of his bluster right then and there.

"Yes, his name is Simba, and we've been together for ten years." His voice lost all of its highfalutin style, and he suddenly became down-to-earth pet daddy.

"Awww. Hi, Simba." April stroked the dog's silky fur.

"He needs to be brushed." The last was said apologetically as if the poor dog were neglected, and I assure you he did not seem to be. Quite the contrary. Simba seemed very well cared for and well-groomed.

The Shih Tzu name comes from a Chinese word which means lion, and the dogs were originally bred to resemble the Chinese lions depicted in traditional Oriental art. In the 1930s they were introduced in England and were nicknamed the Chrysanthemum Dog.

Simba was a classic Shih Tzu with the long coat, adorable face, and dark inquisitive eyes, and from all appearances, Simba was in love. He'd accepted a few pets from April Mae, then had trotted back to his doggie bed, unearthed what must have been a favorite toy and carried it to her.

"Well, will you look at him." April Mae laughed. "Thank you, you handsome guy."

Simba was a delightful dog. I'd had a few clients with Shih Tzus, but as a rule they're amiable canines. First and foremost they're a companion, and the only issue I've seen much is separation anxiety. They don't like to be separated from their humans. Which could be why Philippe brought Simba to the gallery with him.

While April Mae continued to talk to Philippe and Simba, I continued to walk the gallery. I noticed a grouping of paintings by Clive, the one-named artist, who'd been at Kitty's funeral.

The grouping was called "Survival" and there were several abstracts all created in sort of jungle colors. They were good, but in a disturbing sort of way.

Philippe appeared at my side. "He's a local artist."

"He does well?"

He hesitated and then finally said, "An inconsistent talent, I'm afraid."

"What do you mean by that?" I wasn't sure artistic talent was supposed to be a churn-out-the-next-one kind of thing. Painting wasn't the same as making a widget. Creativity flows. Sometimes it ebbs and flows.

"Well, for instance," Philippe clarified, "these are very good, but then he had a dry spell where he could produce nothing at all."

"Really?" I wondered at Philippe's sharing of this insider-type intel. I didn't think his information was a very good sales technique unless he was trying to convince me the paintings were rare.

"Now, it seems Clive is painting again." Philippe waved his hand dismissively and turned from the collection to look at me. "I understand from April Mae you believe I had a disagreement with Kitty Bardot the day before she died."

I guess April had decided I was to be the

"bad cop." I glared at her, but she was so absorbed playing with Simba that my disapproval was wasted.

"We," I emphasized the "we" part, "had been told you and Kitty had an argument."

"That's true."

"So, you admit you had harsh words."

"I don't know about harsh, but we yelled at each other." He shrugged. "Something we did frequently, I'm afraid."

I waited for him to explain.

"Ms. Bardot was fierce about her clients. A good thing for them, I think. But not always good for the person on the other end of things. Like me. We didn't always see eye to eye on what I, as the gallery owner, thought was appropriate and what she as the publicist wanted."

"I see."

"It doesn't mean I didn't respect her. She was top-notch. If I needed PR, she was who I would hire."

I sighed. He sure didn't sound like he'd been so mad at her that he'd kill her. But Philippe was the first real lead we'd had.

Not that we had leads or were investigating or anything. Just in case Malone asks.

April Mae reluctantly left Simba and joined us. "If you hear anything, will you let us know?" She fished a piece of paper from her purse and wrote down a number. "Here's my phone number."

The gallery owner took the paper.

"And if you ever need a dog-sitter, I'm your girl."

Philippe pocketed the note with a smile. "I'll keep that in mind."

April Mae smiled back.

"I have a couple of Tobey and Minou's paintings. Did you see them?"

"No, but I'd love to." She took his arm, and they headed over to another showroom. "Come on, Caro."

Just then my cell phone rang, so I begged off following them. It was a prospective client with a little Papillon rescue who was chewing everything in sight. I made arrangements to meet the family and the culprit the following day.

I finished my call as Philippe and April Mae returned.

"Well, once you've experimented a little with the cats and their painting, and you're ready for an evaluation, give me a call. I can stop by the house." Philippe handed April Mae his business card.

"I'll do that." She waved the card at him and then opened her purse and dropped it in. "Ready, Caro?"

As we walked back to the car, we discussed

Philippe and the gallery. We were in agreement about the slim chance he could be involved in Kitty's death.

Also, for the record, I want it noted I mentioned again the need to follow-up with Detective Malone.

CHAPTER FOURTEEN

The next day was another busy one with appointments throughout the morning. I'd left the afternoon free to help with an ARL donation pick up. April Mae had offered the loan of her pickup so we could haul the large pet food contribution.

As I turned into my drive and hit the remote to put my car in the garage, I noted April Mae's truck was gone. Hopefully she wasn't out asking questions. She'd been tickled with the idea our undercover experience with Philippe Arman the day before had gone well. Although the pretense had lasted all of maybe five minutes. I hoped she'd passed the information on to Detective Malone and let it go. I knew from experience the problems created from sticking your nose in other people's murder investigations.

I also hoped she'd remembered I was borrowing her truck and she would be back soon.

Don Furry and I were to pick up the donated pet food from a pet store that was about to close. It was a great deal for the Laguna Beach animal shelter. In an affluent community like ours, you'd think the shelter wouldn't struggle, and we'd have great support. And we did have a ton of donor support, but every dollar we didn't have to spend, meant we could stretch those donations further.

I went inside to change, and when I checked again, the truck was back.

I'd worn my Protecting Unwanted Pets T-shirt, this time with cargo shorts. I'd brought home a PUP T-shirt for April Mae. I'd planned to give it to her to thank her for the use of her truck, but now that I looked at it I thought it was way too big. The shop had children's sizes; I would have to try one of those.

I walked across the front lawn and rang the doorbell.

April Mae answered clad in an over-sized T-shirt. Sounds pretty tame, right.

But this shirt had a cartoon graphic of a shapely woman in a bikini top and a grass skirt. April Mae's curly blonde head looked unnaturally small atop Hula Girl's . . . ah, assets. Yeah, I needed to work on getting that PUP T-shirt in her size.

"You won't believe what I found out today." The pitch of her voice was even higher than usual with excitement.

"What?"

"Well, I went down the police station to talk to your detective, and I told him what we'd found out from that Philippe guy, but he was not at all forthcoming with any information of his own."

"Hmmm." I'd been through that conversation.

"Then I went to the gas station to gas up my truck so you and your friend from the animal shelter wouldn't have to worry about it."

"That was nice, April Mae, sugar, but you didn't need to do that."

"Well, Tom is kinda leaking oil."

"Tom?"

"Yeah, Tom, that's what I call my truck. He works better if you talk nice to him. I don't know if you noticed the spots on the driveway. Tom's drooling a bit more than normal. I'm afraid he's on his last legs. I hope he'll last until I can get him fixed or maybe replaced if my inheritance is enough."

I had noticed the large dark spots on the

driveway but hadn't really thought much about what was causing them. As for her inheritance, I was pretty sure it was enough.

"Anyway, I asked the cute guy inside the gas station for a rag, so I could check the oil and see if it was low, and he came out to do it for me. Wasn't that sweet of him? Anyway, he noticed my out-of-state license plates and asked what I was doing in town. I told him about me and my sister. And he said, 'Is that the rich lady who got shot?' and I said, 'I didn't know that Sissy was all that rich but she was the one that got shot.' And then he said, 'I guess they think it was the Russian mob what shot her.' "

She took a breath. I was glad because I was getting dizzy from trying to follow her gestures, let alone her logic.

"The Russian mob? Why would the Russian mob shoot Kitty?"

"Caro, honey, that's what I said too. But he'd heard it from this other guy what works there, and he heard it from his cousin who works at the police department." Her blue eyes were as big as beach balls. "Can you believe the Russian mob? Russia's a long ways away. What the heck are they even doing in California?"

"I don't know."

"Anyway, hon, here's the keys, and it's got

130

gas. And I topped off the oil, and he let me keep the oil rag. It's under the seat in case you need it."

Tobey and Minou appeared behind April.

"Hi there, you gorgeous and talented kitties." She reached down and scratched behind Minou's ears which brought an immediate purr. "We are going to try some painting this afternoon. I found all the supplies, and I think it might be soothing for them."

"I won't be long."

"No hurry. Take your time. We'll be busy."

I jingled the keys in my hand as I walked to the truck. Who knew if the cats would find painting soothing, but it would keep them busy. And it would be something for April Mae to do other than refine her detecting skills and get me in trouble with Malone. It wasn't me doing the investigating, but somehow I knew he'd think I had encouraged her. And then I'd be in trouble.

Putting the key in the ignition, I turned it, and the pickup started. It chugged a little to begin with and then the engine seemed to even out. April had suggested talking to it would help, but I wasn't sure I spoke Ford.

I patted the dashboard. "Tom, don't you give me any trouble, buddy." I hoped Tom held out for April Mae until the estate was settled. I had no idea how long something like that took, and I didn't know what kind of money Kitty'd had, but her house alone was worth quite a bit. It was clear April Mae had no idea what kind of money she was about to come into.

I picked up Don Furry at the ARL, and we headed out of town. This store was just outside of Irvine and not too far. Stam and Camille Kabal, the couple who'd owned it, were pet lovers and had been foster parents to some of our more difficult rescues. The shop wasn't closing because of lack of business. They'd made a good go of it, but were retiring to move back east to be closer to their children and grandchildren. When they'd called to offer the pet food donation, we were thrilled. We knew it was good nutritional food, but the challenge had been a way to get it picked up. April's offer of her pickup had been a godsend.

I backed the truck up to the rear of the building. The store was no longer open, but they'd said they would meet us.

When I turned the pickup off, a dark puff of smoke erupted from the exhaust.

"Come on, Tom," I said. "Really?"

Don looked at me like I'd lost my mind.

"April Mae named her truck Tom. She says it helps to talk to him."

"I hope Tom is feeling cooperative today." Don didn't seem convinced conversation was the key.

"April says it uses oil."

"Hello, Caro. Hello, Don." Stam had come outside. "Come in. I'm real sorry I'm not able to help you load, but my back is iffy at best."

"No problem," Don said. "We can handle the loading."

It took some muscle, but we got the big bags of dog food into the truck. One of the bags broke open in the process, and I cleaned up the spillage while Don went to let Stam and Camille know we were done. I hoped when we got to the animal shelter there'd be a few more helping hands to assist with the unload. I'd finished my clean up when Don came back outside.

"Maybe we should check the oil just to be sure," he suggested. "I'd hate to cause further problems than this guy already has." He patted the hood of the truck. "Right, Tom?"

"Okay. April checked it earlier and said she left a rag inside the cab. We can stop and get some oil if we need to."

Don opened the passenger door and rooted around the seat to find the rag. I made sure the tailgate was closed tightly.

"Caro," Don's voice was muffled with his head inside the cab.

"Yes?"

"I think you need to come here."

"Coming." I'd made sure everything was secure in the back and nothing would blow out.

"What?"

Don stepped back from the side of the truck and motioned to me. "I think you'd better see this." He pulled the passenger seat forward.

Nestled behind it was a rifle.

It was a quiet drive back to Laguna Beach. Don and I were both so rattled we hadn't bothered to check the oil after all.

I headed straight to the shelter, and once we'd unloaded the bags of dog food, I debated whether I should simply drive to the police station and show Malone or go home and call him.

Neither Don nor I had touched the gun.

There could be a good reason April had a rifle. I couldn't think of a good reason, but there had to be one.

Still a rifle. A dead woman. A big inheritance. It wasn't going to look good.

I tried Malone on my cell phone before I left the shelter and got his voicemail. I left an urgent message with a heavy heart. I'd gotten attached to the little sprite, and I really wanted to just ask her about the gun. But if I did that and then the gun was gone before Malone could check it out, that could be a problem. A big problem.

I decided I would go directly to the Laguna Beach police station. It's downtown, not far off Laguna Canyon Road. In fact, very near my office.

I parked out front and walked into the building.

"Lorraine, is Detective Malone in?" I asked the woman at the desk.

"No, Caro. He's out doing his detecting thing." Now you might ask how I was on a first name basis with the clerk at the Laguna Beach PD. And it would be a good question. Suffice to say, we'd spent some time together when my friend, Diana, had been wrongly accused of a crime.

"Do you know when he'll be back?"

"I'm not sure. Do you want me to give him a message?"

"I left a message on his cell phone but yes, if he shows up, tell him I need to see him, and it's urgent."

"Will do, hon." She went back to her paperwork.

"Thanks." I went back outside to the truck. I needed to plug the parking meter again. I searched through my purse for change. Dang, the coins I'd used before must have been it.

My cell phone rang, and I could see it was April Mae's number. I didn't answer.

I climbed back in the truck and started it. There was a puff of dark smoke as the engine turned over, and I remember Don and I had never checked the oil.

I popped the hood open and retrieved the oily rag from the passenger side. The rag that'd started this whole mess.

Sure enough, Tom was already a quart low. That must be some oil leak. Maybe April Mae was right, and he was on his last legs . . . er . . . tires. Poor Tom.

I closed the hood. Shoot, I'd gotten oil all over my hands. I wiped them on the rag but it was so dirty it was a lost cause. I finally just wiped them on my shorts.

I thought about going back into the police station. But knew I'd get a parking ticket for sure if I left the truck parked at an expired meter. Well, while I was waiting for Malone to call back I could stop by the service station and put in some oil. It would give me something to do other than wait for the busy detective and avoid April Mae's calls. Maybe I could wash my hands while I was there.

I pulled out onto Forest and headed for the Mobil station on PCH. Just as I turned onto Beach Street, I noted the flashing lights in the rearview mirror. I pulled over so the police car could pass. The blue and white car and its flashing lights pulled in behind me.

What the heck?

The officer came to my window. "Ma'am, are you aware you have a broken taillight?"

"No, I wasn't aware. The truck isn't mine. It's a friend's. I'll be sure to let her know."

"I need to see your license and registration, ma'am."

Oh, okay, he probably needed to write me a warning. Great. I'd avoided the forty-dollar parking ticket only to get a faulty equipment ticket. I wondered what those went for.

I opened the glove box, and a large hunting knife and a box of ammo fell out.

I looked at the officer to see if he'd noticed.

He had.

"Please step out of the car, ma'am."

"I can explain." Even I knew how lame that sounded.

"Step out —"

"Okay, officer, I'm getting out." I opened the door, climbed out and handed him my license. "If you would just call Detective Judd Malone."

"Malone in homicide?" he asked. "Why, have you killed someone?"

"What? No. Do I look like a killer?"

He started to say something.

"Don't answer that question." I pointed my finger at him. My grimy digit within inches of Officer Gung-ho's fresh face.

Just then my cell phone rang from inside my purse which was still in the truck. "Can I answer my phone? It's either Malone or April Mae, the owner of the truck, wondering why I don't have it back yet."

"No."

The ringing stopped and then started again immediately. So, it was probably April Mae.

"Please just contact Detective Malone. I've been trying to reach him."

"Ma'am, I need you to walk back to the squad car with me." This young guy was serious, and I couldn't help but think this could not be going much worse.

Then worse arrived.

Malone pulled up behind the police cruiser and got out. "Officer Hostas." He nodded to his colleague and then turned to me. "Ms. Lamont." Then crossed his arms in typical Malone stance. "Would someone like to fill me in?"

The officer let me speak first. I explained about borrowing April's truck, the oil leak, the discovery of the rifle, and my attempts to reach him. Officer Hostas finished up with the traffic stop.

I thought we made a great team.

"Okay, show me the rifle." Malone addressed me.

I walked to the passenger side pulled the seat forward and moved so Malone could see. Yep, big ole rifle. Still right where I last saw it.

Malone didn't touch it. "All right, we're going to impound the vehicle," he said to Officer Hostas. "You call it in."

Detective Malone turned to me. "You and who else were in the truck?"

"Don Furry from the Laguna Animal Rescue."

"We'll need his fingerprints. We already have yours on file."

The uniformed officer raised one brow and looked at me as if to say, *I knew you were a criminal.*

"Not because I did anything wrong," I said. "Because they were needed to eliminate me as a suspect."

The brow went higher. *A suspect, huh? Still suspicious if you ask me.*

Before I could explain away his suspicions about me, Malone interrupted. "Officer Hostas? The impound? Would you call it in?"

The young officer walked back to his car presumably to make the requested call.

"When he gets back I'm going to have him take you home. You can get your bag out of the truck." Malone motioned to the still open door. "All you need to tell Ms. Bardot's sister is you were stopped, the rifle was found, and I'll be in touch."

Officer Hostas returned from his cruiser, and Malone explained he was charged with taking me home. He still looked at me like I might be a serial killer but didn't argue.

Don't try anything funny. I'm keeping an eye on you. He opened the back passenger door of the squad car for me politely, but his thoughts came through loud and clear.

This was the first time I'd ever been in a police cruiser. It's not a pleasant experience. Even in Laguna Beach where the cars are pretty new and the crimes are pretty petty, the backseat didn't smell so good. Then there was also the fact there were no door handles. No way to let yourself out. Creepy.

The officer pulled up in my driveway, and as he did I noticed a light blue Ferrari.

Holy Crap. I'd forgotten I had a date with Sam Gallanos. Sam was there to pick me up. Right on time.

I, however, was not on time.

Sam leaned against the car seemingly enjoying the late afternoon sun. Cool and collected. Attired in lightweight tan chinos, his white linen shirt showed his tan to perfection. He looked like he'd just walked out of a magazine ad.

I was sweaty and covered in dust. I still wore my PUP T-shirt and now filthy cargo shorts. Classy. Oh, and I was arriving in a police cruiser.

Nice.

My mama would be appalled.

Heck, I was appalled.

The officer got out and opened the door for me. I thanked him for the ride and waved as he drove away.

Yeah, I was stalling.

"Hi." Sam was right there when I turned around. He'd pushed his sunglasses up, and his dark eyes held back humor. Just barely.

I was hyper-aware I looked like something the dog wouldn't even have bothered to drag in. Grime and dust from the loading, dog food smell from the spill, grease from checking Tom's oil. I could not have looked or smelled worse if I'd tried.

Sam, undaunted, leaned forward and kissed me on my grimy cheek. "Complications?"

"Yeah, kind of," I sighed. "Sam, I'm so sorry. I got caught up in, well, I — ah." I couldn't even put words to the afternoon I'd just spent.

"No worries. With you, Caro, there are always complications. You're a complicated woman." His smile said he knew there'd be an explanation in due time.

"I have to go next door and explain to April Mae why I'm not returning her truck to her."

"Do you want me to come or wait here?"

"Oh, hell, Sam. You might as well come. It will fill in a lot without me having to say it twice."

We trekked across my front yard to April Mae's. I rang the bell and waited. When April Mae came to the door she was covered in paint. To be absolutely accurate, the hula girl on her T-shirt was the one covered in paint splotches. Paw-shaped splotches.

I couldn't help but smile. "Looks like they painted you."

"Yeah, more me than the pictures." She giggled.

"Maybe their artistic temperaments aren't ready to paint yet."

"Could be, but I think the big problem is their claws. They pretty much shredded the canvas I gave them to work on."

"Their claws should probably be trimmed. Kitty kept them pretty short. She did it herself, but if you need help I could recommend a groomer." Yeah, I was stalling again.

April Mae looked down at her legs, covered in splotches of paints and scratches. "I think I need help. You mentioned you had a friend?"

"I'll get you Kendall's number," I told her. *Right after I explain that the police have your truck. And your gun. And your knife.*

"That'd be great!"

"The cats are painting again," I said to Sam.

April Mae suddenly noticed Sam behind me, and like most females there was a sudden change in her. I liken it to the heightened awareness Dogbert gets when he smells a pork chop. Or my mama gets when she hears there's a sale at Neiman Marcus. Dogbert actually drools. Mama just drools internally, but the look in their eyes is the same.

"April Mae, honey, there was a problem with your truck, and the police have impounded it." I decided I'd start with the basics.

"Who is that?" She pointed at Sam.

"That's Sam." I moved slightly to the side. "April Mae, my friend, Sam. Sam, April Mae Wooben, Kitty's sister."

She giggled and waved at him.

"Nice to meet you." Sam kept it formal.

"April Mae, Detective Malone will be calling you in a little bit about Tom."

"Tom?" It must have finally sunk in. She looked behind me. "But, Caro, where is Tom?"

"Tom is her truck," I explained to Sam.

"Where is my truck?"

"That's what I'm trying to explain, sugar." If the girl would just focus instead of standing there like a bump on a log, drooling over Sam. "Close your mouth."

"Huh?"

"Come on," I said to her. "Let's go inside for a minute."

Tobey and Minou appeared the minute we walked into the living room. Thank God, April Mae'd had the good sense to clean them up. They'd already met Sam, so they were not as awestruck as their mistress.

Sam remembered the cats from the night Kitty'd died. He made over them, and they preened. Sam was one of those people who seemed to be comfortable anywhere. He settled into one of the chairs, and Minou situated herself on his lap.

I tried to get April Mae to focus enough for me to explain about finding the rifle, getting stopped, Laguna Beach PD impounding the truck.

At the point where I'd explained about the officer asking if I'd killed someone, I think Sam might have snorted, but like Walt, when I looked at him, he had this innocent neutral look on his face.

"So I loaned you my truck, and now it's impounded, and they think I killed my very own sister?"

Yeah, that about summed it up. The facts had finally sunk in, and the realization had hit April Mae she had some things to clear up with the local police.

April Mae's cell phone rang, and she jumped.

"I'm sure that will be Detective Malone with questions for you." I said quickly. "I'm going to go home and clean up, and I'll talk to you later."

I headed for the front door and could hear Sam saying good-bye to April Mae as I headed out.

He'd caught up with me by the time I reached my front door.

"I'm sorry, Sam." I brushed at my legs, which were covered in dog food dust. "I'm afraid I'm going to have to take a rain check."

"Caro, I have an idea." He reached past me and pushed open the door. "Let's try this."

I tried not to get him dirty as I ducked under his arm.

"How about I take Dogbert for a walk while you shower. I'm sure he needs some exercise."

He was right, poor Dog had been cooped up all day.

"Just throw on something comfortable, and we'll forgo dinner and take a little walk on the beach. Sounds like you could use a little decompression time."

I sighed. It sounded like heaven to me. I nodded assent and headed down the hallway to clean up my look and hopefully my attitude.

When I got out of the shower, I dressed in capris, a bright flower-print jersey tank top and walking shoes. My hair was still a bit out of control, but there was no taming it in such a short time, so I simply pulled it back and tied a scarf around the ponytail. The scarf made me think of both Tonya Miles and Clive the artist.

Sam had just returned from his walk with Dogbert.

"Don't tell him we're going to the beach or he'll want to go." I laughed.

"I know. If Mac finds out I've been on the beach, and especially with you, my name will be mud."

Mac was Sam's Border Collie. A gorgeous guy in his own right, and Border Collies were a favorite of mine.

"It's okay. I can keep a secret." I smiled at Sam. And then realized what I'd said.

"Well, I don't know whether or not that's true based on what I just heard next door."

We started at Main Beach and walked south. Sam had bought us each a frozen yogurt at Chantilly's when he parked the car. The beach was dotted with other walkers and a few evening surfers and skimboarders.

Sam had rolled up his pant legs, and we walked at the edge of the water where we could. The sound of the surf was restful, and Sam seemed to know I needed time to sort out the chaos in my brain.

We'd gone quite a ways down the beach when I stopped.

"Ready to turn back?" he asked.

"Yes." I was suddenly completely exhausted.

We turned back to Main Beach and once

there settled on a bench.

"April Mae is going to be pretty upset with me." I brushed at the sand on the bench.

"She put you in an awful position, Caro. She'll have to understand you had no choice."

"Yeah, I guess." I'd been over all of it in my head, and I didn't see any other options. I'd done what I thought I had to do.

"The police seem no closer to solving Kitty Bardot's murder." Sam stretched out his legs and leaned back against the bench, sliding his sunglasses back on.

"That's why I'm afraid they'll latch onto this. I'd heard they have video of the shooter from the Time Keeper's security camera."

"That would seem to make sense. There are cameras everywhere these days." He extended his arm toward the Main Beach lifeguard tower. "There are probably several on us right now."

"A comment, I'm afraid, of the times we live in."

"You seem pretty convinced Kitty's sister isn't a true suspect. Are you sure about her?"

"Very sure. Don't get me wrong, she's got issues. More issues than a magazine stand. But unless she's an incredible actress, I don't think she realized how much money her sister had."

"Hmmm." Sam laced his hands behind his head.

"To tell you the truth, I'm a little worried about her."

"When you think the time is right, I'll give you the name of my financial advisor to pass on," he said. "If she doesn't have someone reputable helping her, there are those who will eat her alive."

"You're right. That would be great, Sam. I should have thought to recommend someone to her."

"No worries. It will be a while before she's ready."

We sat in silence for a few minutes.

I shifted so I was leaning back like Sam. "I keep rolling all this around in my head, and I still can't believe someone would want to kill Kitty."

"You're good at this. Any thoughts yourself on who may have wanted Kitty dead?"

"None at all. Diana told us Kitty'd had a fight with Philippe Arman."

"Arman Gallery, right?"

"Yes, he was the gallery showing the cat's paintings."

"I don't remember seeing him the night of the event at the Montage. The night Kitty was killed."

"I don't either, but he must have been there."

"One would think."

"Whatever call Kitty took before asking me to take the cats home, upset her. And it's what caused her to be on PCH and in the line of fire."

"I'm sure the police have checked her cell phone records."

"I'm sure you're right. But they're not sharing that information with me."

"No, I imagine not." He smiled.

"What if it was April Mae? What if she called Kitty, and then Kitty went to meet her, and she shot her?" I shook my head even as I said it. "No, that's too crazy. I truly believe she'd give up any amount of money to be able to meet her sister in person."

"Who else could it be?"

"That's just it, Sam. I can't think of anyone else."

We sat and talked until the sun went down. Then we just leaned back and enjoyed the view, Sam's arm cushioning my shoulders.

Laguna Beach sunsets were on the list of my favorite things in the whole world. Sam Gallanos was quickly becoming an entry on that list as well. He had such a calming effect on my psyche, always seemed to know just what I needed at the time. Still, I was a little worried about Sam becoming a bigger part of my life. You see, I was pretty sure Sam was a player. A luxury lifestyle, a penchant for fast cars. How long before he'd get bored?

Still, maybe it was enough that we were good together. For now.

CHAPTER FIFTEEN

When I walked into my office building the next day there was a new temp at the desk, and Detective Malone was parked in one of the lobby chairs waiting for me. I didn't have a good feeling about either development.

This temp was an improvement over the last one in understanding our office procedures, but looked like she'd swallowed a lemon. I introduced myself. She told me her name was Sally Purser.

Not sure who kicked her kennel, but Sally was not happy to see me, she was not happy to hand over my messages, she didn't look like she'd been happy any time in the last decade. Maybe longer.

Still, the waiting room was clean and tidy and thankfully empty. No zoo-like atmosphere, so perhaps I could learn to live with the sour lemon face.

"Do you have a pet? A dog or a cat?" I

found sometimes even the toughest characters could be cracked if you could get them
to talk about their animals. Sally might be
the exception. She looked like she'd really
like to tell me it was none of my business.

"Can't stand 'em. Too smelly." She went
back to sorting mail.

I looked at Malone. He shrugged and followed me into my office. Malone wore his
usual — black jeans, black T-shirt, black
leather. Bad-ass attitude.

I'd also dressed in my usual. Jeans to make
it easier if I needed to sit on someone's floor
or lawn, and whatever top I grabbed. This
was a fun yellow Balmain cut-in tank that I
liked a lot. It was easy, wash and wear,
didn't show pet fur. Important attributes.
My mother continually sent me suggestions,
hoping to reform me. It was good Mama
was hundreds of miles away in Texas, or
there'd definitely be more than my wardrobe
she want to improve.

I flipped through my messages while
Malone seated himself in one of the plum-
toned leather chairs. I dropped the notes on
my desk and sat down in the matching chair
opposite his.

"April Mae Wooben's gun permit checks
out. The gun has not been fired recently.
While it's the same type of weapon used to

shoot Ms. Bardot, it appears she uses it as a hunting rifle. Also, Ms. Wooben got a ticket for a broken tail light in Arizona the day her sister was shot."

I could relate to the faulty broken tail light. But wow, that was a lot of information for Malone to share.

"She's still pretty unhappy with me," I noted.

"You did the right thing."

"I know, but I still feel lousy about it."

"You probably owe the older guy at the animal place an apology too," Malone noted.

"Don Furry? Oh my." I'd forgotten he had to be fingerprinted too. "Did you explain to Officer Hostas that I'm not a crazed killer?"

"I did, but he's still not convinced." There was a faint smirk at the corner of Malone's mouth.

"How's the investigation going otherwise?"

"Fine."

"It sounds like April Mae inherits most of the estate. But then you probably already knew that, huh?"

"We did."

"Any luck with the security camera footage?"

Malone didn't answer.

"Okay, I get it. None of my business."

He leaned forward in his chair. "Truthfully, a pretty frustrating investigation. No known enemies. The call the vic took. You said she had an emergency?"

"That's what Kitty said, something urgent she had to take care of right away. She seemed upset."

"She didn't say who called?"

"No, she didn't. Her cell phone records were no help?"

"Nope." He stood. "I'll be in touch."

I gathered the files I needed for the afternoon. I'd stop by home for lunch to give Dogbert a midday break, and then I had a full afternoon. I stopped at the front desk to remind Sourpuss, I mean Sally Purser, I wouldn't be back in the office until the next morning. She could forward anything that couldn't wait to my cell phone.

"I see most of my clients in their own homes," I made sure to clarify.

She didn't even bother to hide her eye roll. "While you were with the detective, a lady called about her dog, Bitty, who her husband picks on. I told her you don't handle animal abuse cases, and she should call animal control at the police department."

"What?" I sputtered. The call could be

the woman from the other day. Diana's next door neighbor. "Did she leave her name?"

"She did not."

"If she calls back, I want to talk to her. Give her my cell number." I left before I lost my cool with the woman.

As soon as I got home and had taken care of Dogbert, I called the office management group who'd arranged the temp services. They assured me the current temp had come highly recommended. It was also what they'd said about the last one. In LaKeesha's defense, no one had explained the process. Sourpuss was a different story; I simply thought the person taking calls, opening mail, and greeting people could be efficient and pleasant.

Okay, on to the animal issues. Sometimes easier to deal with. Make that, always easier to deal with.

I'd checked in with Nicky Chang and her misbehaving Chihuahua, and she said the exercise had already helped a lot. I left her some material about the Chihuahua temperament. She seemed willing to do what was necessary to help Sunny adjust.

Next up was Dexter, a young tan and white beagle, one of the dogs from the circus the other day in the office. I'd promised a free first consultation to everyone who'd been inconvenienced by mistakenly being told to come into the office, and I was working my way through the list.

Dexter's family was at the end of their rope because the little guy kept running and running. He was either asleep or running, creating all kinds of disruption to the household. No one could walk inside without being tripped, and the kids couldn't play in the yard without the beagle racing through whatever they were trying to do. Dexter was a rescue, and I loved they'd taken him on, but it was clear they hadn't understood his need for activity and their own household's need for quiet.

I prescribed daily exercise and play. Especially play involving smells. Beagles are all about the nose. At least once a week at the dog park should help. I also reminded them that when everyone got home from school and work, they needed to wait until Dexter had calmed down before petting him.

They were very interested in trying my suggestions. I'd do a follow-up in a couple of weeks to see how it was going, but this was one case I felt good about. The initial consultation might be the only visit really needed.

As soon as my appointments for the day

were finished, I swung by Ruby Point. I wondered if Bella had heard anything back from Dr. Daniel on the frail nanny goat. Leave it to Diana to foster a sickly goat. Bella'd not heard back from the vet, but everything else with Diana's menagerie appeared to be going well. She said Diana had called and asked to talk to Mr. Wiggles on the phone. It was clear the connection Diana felt with her pets was a mystery to the woman, but she loved Diana and had accepted that the attachment to her pets went with the territory.

I walked over to the residence next door to Diana's. The Corvette wasn't in the drive, but it could be in the garage. What the hey, I decided to go to the door. I pushed the bell and waited. Nothing. Counted to sixty and tried again. Still nothing.

What to do? As you've probably already figured out, doing nothing is dang hard for me. Bottom line, I knew what I'd seen and heard, but I was operating on suppositions. And there's a line where your business ends and somebody else's business begins. I'd offered the help; I would have to wait to hear from her.

I decided to run by the animal shelter and make my apologies to Don Furry and check on Zilla, Rawnsley, and the rest. Hopefully, they'd been adopted but if not, I could take them for a run. Some kind of action would be good for them and for me.

I parked and went in.

"Is Don here?" I asked Nancy, one of the volunteers.

"No, he had to go down to the police station for something, so he left early today."

I felt guilty though I'm not sure why. Like Sam said, April Mae had left the rifle in the truck. Not me.

I checked on the status of Zilla and Rawnsley, but a couple of the other volunteers had just left for the dog park with them. They had been properly socialized with the other shelter residents, and so a run in the park would be great. They could romp and play with the other dogs. Zilla would do great with the Lab bloodlines. Rawnsley, on the other hand, could be a problem. Not in an aggressive sort of way, but in a roaming sort of way. The Great Pyrenees is a gentle breed, but as guardian dogs they're often used to tend sheep, they like to patrol their perimeter, and the volunteers would need to keep an eye on him. The Laguna Beach Dog Park was not fenced on all sides, relying on the terrain for containment.

Of course, they knew all that. I hoped.

Okay, I'd put it off long enough. I needed to go home, clean up, and see if I could repair things with April Mae.

I'd picked up the child-sized PUP T-shirt for April Mae while I was there, stopped off for some flowers, and when I got home stirred up some kitty cookies for Tobey and Minou. Then I went next door.

The April Mae who came to the door was not the sprite I knew and loved. This was a subdued April Mae who had me wishing for the craziness of "You can call me June" days.

"Hi, Caro." She stepped aside to let me in.

That was at least a good sign. She'd let me inside.

"These are for you." I handed her the flowers and the T-shirt. "And these," I produced the plate of kitty cookies, "are for Tobey and Minou. I'm sorry."

"Ahhh, Caro. You did what you thought you needed to do." Her eyes filled with tears. "No apology is necessary."

Then April Mae hugged me, and I knew things would be okay.

The next day, I was almost afraid to go into the office and find out what temp we had today. I stopped by the Koffee Klatch for my usual latte, screwed up my courage, and headed to PAWS.

We still had Sourpuss. I mean, Sally Purser. Now I'd messed with her name so often in my head, I had to be careful I didn't say the nickname out loud. Sally P. was again not happy to see me.

I took a few minutes before I started the day to give Kendall Reese a call. Kendall was a dog-groomer at the local Divine Pet Spa and a friend. I knew Kendall'd be perfect to help April Mae with getting Tobey and Minou's claws under control.

It was great to talk to Kendall. I hadn't seen him since the last time I'd taken Dogbert in, and I missed his fun and flamboyant personality. I explained about April Mae and the cats and asked if he'd help.

"You got it, girlfriend!" He made me promise we'd get together soon.

I gave my word and said I'd have April Mae give him a call. Kendall was a joy. Maybe we could get together at the Dog Park. His Pomeranian, Guido, and my mutt, Dogbert. That would be fun.

I continued to smile as I walked through the lobby on the way to my morning appointments.

Sally P. appeared affronted by my good humor.

The rest of the day went quickly. I loved my work, and for the first time since Kitty's death, I felt like things were beginning to feel normal again.

CHAPTER SIXTEEN

I had just gotten home when all of a sudden there was loud honking. I parked my car in the garage and stepped outside. April Mae had just pulled into the driveway next door.

In a Cadillac convertible. A humongous black older-model Cadillac convertible.

April Mae's tiny arm waved like she was in a homecoming parade. (Believe me, I know. Part of Texas beauty pageant training is parade waves.)

"What do you think?" She parked the tank-like car and then jumped out all smiles. Apparently, she'd really decided to forgive me for the gun incident.

I walked toward her. What I thought was that it was one heck of a big car for such a tiny woman. Seriously, could she even see over the steering wheel?

"It's huge." I couldn't think of anything else.

"I know! Don't you just love it?"

"It's — ah — it's — nice." I couldn't destroy her obvious enthusiasm for the big tank.

"Come on over, I've got takeout, and I'm happy to share." She pulled a big bag from the Shake Shack out of the backseat. "That's where I met Johnny, the guy who was sellin' this baby." She patted the shiny black fender. "It was a steal."

I sincerely hoped it really wasn't in the literal sense, but feared it could be. There was something so pimpmobile about it.

As I'd gotten closer, I'd realized the car wasn't the only thing different.

"Uhmm . . . April Mae," I stammered. "What have you done with your hair?"

Her blonde locks had been smoothed and dyed in the same rosette pattern as Tobey and Minou's fur. While the splotches and glittering were perfect on the cats, on April Mae the look could only be called bizarre.

"It's — ah — it's — nice."

There I was, lying again in order to keep from crushing her child-like enthusiasm. April Mae Wooben had turned me into a pathological liar.

"Your friend, Kendall, helped me with Tobey and Minou's nail trimmin'. Then he took me to his hairstylist, and it took hours, but Ricki was able to do this." April Mae touched her hands to her head of Bengal fur-patterned hair. "Then Kendall took me shopping."

My brain worked hard to assimilate the new car, the new hair, and the idea of Kendall and April Mae shopping together.

"How is Kendall?"

"He is so funny." She giggled. "And you haven't been honest with me, girlfriend."

Yep, she sounded like she'd spent the day with Kendall. About what had I not been honest, I wondered. That her hair was ridiculous? That her car was a pimpmobile? That Kendall was gay?

"Kendall tells me you're quite the detective your own self. He said when Diana Knight was arrested, you were the one who figured it out, and the police had to let her go."

Well, it hadn't been quite as simple as Kendall represented it, but I had put together some of the pieces of the puzzle. Unfortunately, not soon enough, and I'd found myself face to face with the killer. Which may have been why Malone was so insistent I mind my own business.

Speaking of Detective Malone.

Detective Malone and his silver Camaro rolled into the driveway and parked behind

April Mae's big black Cadillac. He got out and approached us. His walk said, "I'm bad," with no words needed. As he got closer, the swagger slowed and his face stayed tough guy, but I could tell Malone was as distracted by April Mae's hair as I was. It was like a train wreck. You couldn't look away.

"June . . . ah, ma'am." He apparently had decided to give up on what to call her. "We've been given some information from the Los Angeles Police Department about a complaint that your sister and three other publicists filed. They had received death threats."

"Oh, no. Somebody threatened Sissy?"

"We believe that's the case, and we're working cooperatively with the LAPD. The other three received additional threats after the complaint was filed. Did you see anything in your sister's mail? Any unusual correspondence? Letters with foreign postmarks?"

"I don't think so." April Mae placed a finger on her cheek as she thought, and I realized Kendall's stylist had also provided a manicure. April's very long nails, dare I say "claws", had been polished a deep gleaming black.

I felt guilty. I'd been the one who'd

facilitated the relationship.

"We can look if you want." She headed toward the front door. "Come on."

Detective Malone shrugged and then came as called. I trailed behind, my curiosity winning out.

She held open the door, and we ducked in. Tobey and Minou greeted April Mae and then came to greet us brushing against our legs. I reached down to pet both cats. Gorgeous fur. I looked back at April Mae. A better look for them than for her.

"I couldn't open Sissy's mail. I mean, it's not addressed to me, and even though she was my sister, I didn't really know her." She disappeared into the kitchen but kept talking. "It just didn't seem right. So I've just been saving it. The lawyer's been payin' all the bills, and so I guess I thought maybe at some point he might need some of the other mail."

She walked out from the kitchen carrying a laundry basket full of unopened mail.

Oh wow.

"I've got to run home and let Dogbert out, but then I can come back over and help sort if you like," I offered.

"Sure, Caro hon, that would be spiffy." April Mae grinned as she settled herself on the couch with a handful of envelopes.

167

"Here, detective, you can sit right here by me." She patted the cushion beside her.

"The mail will need to go down to the station. The forensics team can go through it, and they'll be able to preserve any fingerprints if we find anything." Malone had on his serious face. "I'll bring the remainder back when they're done."

"Oh." April Mae's disappointment was clear. I wasn't sure whether it had more to do with missing out on any clues or not getting to enjoy close quarters with Malone.

Detective Malone picked up the laundry basket, held it out for April Mae to add the envelopes she held, and then headed toward the door. He turned back to look at me.

"Caro, can I see you outside for a moment."

"Sure." We stepped into the afternoon heat.

"It's about the car." He indicated the black Cadillac.

"What about the car?" It was crazy huge, but I was pretty sure street legal.

"Did April or June or whatever the hell the woman's name is, tell you where she bought the car?"

"Yes, she said it was some guy she met at the Shake Shack. Let me think." Maybe the car really was stolen. "I believe she said the guy's name was Johnny something."

"That's what I thought. Johnny the Hood. The dingbat has bought a car from the mob." He set the laundry basket on the ground and opened his trunk.

"There's no mob in Laguna Beach."

"The hell there's not." Malone placed the basket of mail in his trunk and slammed the lid.

"Johnny the Hood and his associates, Mike the Knife and Shotgun Sal, have been a problem around here for years." Malone's jaw was handsomely unshaven, and he rubbed it in agitation. "We've got all kinds of files on them, but we only seem to be able to get the low-level patsies."

Mob, patsies, crazy mobster names. I felt like I'd been dropped in an Al Capone movie. An Al Capone movie that had been turned into a sit-com.

Only Malone wasn't finding any of this amusing. His crossed arms and legs apart stance let me know this was not the time to try to lighten the mood.

"Okay, so if there is organized crime here in Laguna Beach —" He started to interrupt, but I put my hand up. "Just let me finish, sugar."

He stopped but still looked none too happy.

"Where's the harm in April Mae buying a car from them?" I truly couldn't see the problem. So far as I could tell, they hadn't tried to recruit her, they hadn't tried to kill her. If anything, much like me, they probably felt like protecting her. Like a small defenseless kitten, she brought that out in folks.

"First off, we don't know if they're unloading it because it was used in a crime," Malone bit out. "Secondly, we don't know who they've pissed off that might come after her."

"You think people may think she's associated with them because of the car?" I asked.

"Yes."

"So, what can we do?"

"You can talk her into giving it back," he suggested.

"I can try, hon, but I doubt that's going to happen."

"One more thing." He began to pace. "I don't even believe I'm going to say this." He stopped and looked at me.

"What?"

"I'd like for you to keep an eye on April, er, June, whatever the hell her name is."

I couldn't believe my ears. Malone was asking for my help?

"Caro?" He took me by the shoulders and

raised my chin with the touch of his knuckle, so I had to look him in the eyes.

"Yes." I might have said it a little breathlessly.

"Do not investigate. Do not question people. Do not put her or yourself in danger. Do you understand?"

I nodded.

He dropped his hand from my chin. "All I'm asking you to do is to keep an eye on her, and let me know if anything comes up. Keep me informed. Okay?"

"Okay."

Needless to say, the idea of Malone asking for my assistance amused me to no end. As I walked back to the house, I wondered if that meant I could be classified as "Deputy Lamont" and if I could get a badge.

I didn't think encouraging April Mae to steal from a Laguna Beach business counted as "keeping an eye on her." Or at least, I didn't think Malone would think so. Nevertheless, that's the situation I found myself in at one o'clock the next day.

April Mae and I had decided midday would be the best time to retrieve Grandma Tillie's brooch from cousin Mel. We hoped the Bow Wow Boutique would be busy as it would be easier for April Mae to get in and out unnoticed.

I hoped her skills weren't too rusty. She'd assured me picking the lock and grabbing the brooch would be no problem. My only role was to be the distraction.

We'd parked down the block quite a ways. I'd insisted on driving. It wasn't that I didn't trust April Mae's black pimpmobile, but the honest to goodness fact was there was no way the car would not attract attention.

I went in first. I'd dressed for the occasion, since I knew what I had on would be reported in great detail as the story was told and retold.

My favorite Escada jeans, paired with a brand new ecru Vera Wang silk T-shirt, and a brilliant orange Ferragamo scarf flung around my neck as an accent. I knew it clashed with my hair, but I didn't care. It had been a Christmas gift from my cousin, Mel, a few Christmases ago, and I knew she would recognize it in an instant. I needed to give her plenty to process to make sure her attention stayed on me.

You cannot believe how nervous I was. My hands shook as I pushed open the shop door. A bell jangled as I opened it, announcing my entrance. Mel was with a customer. I recognized the well-known plastic surgeon,

Jack O'Doggle. He didn't have a dog, so he was undoubtedly shopping for a gift. I had to hand it to Mel, she'd made a huge success of the Bow Wow Boutique.

There was a good crowd of people milling around. All the better — the more people who saw me, the fewer who were looking elsewhere.

I walked through to the back of the store where Mel had the dog carriers and pet car seats. I could feel everyone's eyes on me. I kept my head high and eyes straight ahead.

I seldom was glad for all the time I'd wasted learning about posture and carriage, but I'm telling you, sometimes all the years of beauty pageant training comes in handy. There was a titter as I walked through. Whispered comments. I tuned them out.

I positioned myself so I could look through the merchandise and still be seen. I wanted to be in plain sight but didn't want to be able to see April Mae, because I didn't want my face or body language to give away her movements. With luck we'd complete our mission on time, and the realization the brooch was missing would go undiscovered until we were well away.

I picked up a black Italian leather carrier and turned it over in my hands. The leather was soft and supple; the price was more than most folks' car payments. I put the carrier back down and reached for an open straw carrier rimmed in pink silk roses. Cute. It reminded me of Diana, and I wondered if Mr. Wiggles would fit in it. It was definitely small.

A suede dog sling with cheetah faux fur trimming was next. The African feral's fur made me think of April Mae's hair, and I snickered to myself. I'd convinced her that a hat would be a good idea for our foray into crime if she was to get in and out without drawing attention to herself. When she'd shown up at my door, her colorful locks had been stuffed into a baseball cap.

I had to trust she could slip into the store unnoticed.

I glanced at my watch furtively. We'd agreed on ten minutes. Little Miss Petty Thief swore ten minutes was plenty of time.

I leaned down to check out a rolling dog traveler (think suitcase on wheels with mesh so the dog can breathe) and was startled by a face looking at me from the other side. I jumped, banging my head on the display table.

"Hi, Darby."

"Hi, Caro." Darby pushed her blonde curls out of her face.

"How did it go with Mandy Beenerman

and Nietzsche?" I'd referred Mandy and her Lhasa Apso to Darby. I think I mentioned it before — Darby has Paw Prints, the pet photography studio next door to Mel's boutique. Darby was also Mel's greatest defender and her best friend. Oh, and Mel had recently helped clear Darby of a murder rap. Makes for some heavy-duty loyalty.

"Great. Thanks for the recommendation. Nietzsche's a beautiful dog."

From then on, Darby was on me like white on rice. Every move I made, she was there. Eyes narrowed, watching my every move. Always between me and the display case. I risked a glance at my watch again. Time was up.

I took my exit slowly, stopping at a display of cleverly arranged new arrivals on my way toward the front door.

With my hand on the door handle, I glanced back to see where Mel was.

Our eyes met, and I worked hard to keep my face neutral. If there was even a hint of triumph or humor in my expression she would rush to the display case. I needed her to feel safe, to think Darby's vigilance and her watchfulness had thwarted me.

All those years in teen pageants, smiling and saying, "I'm so thrilled for Suzy," or

"I'm so happy to be Miss Runner-Up," paid off.

Poker face. Poker face. No emotion. I held her gaze and waited a full beat.

Mel doesn't have a poker face. Her dark eyes blazed with, "I am not going to look away first."

Okay, cuz. I tried to look defeated. I broke eye contact and looked at the floor, purposely dropped my shoulders, and then I was out the door.

I made myself walk down the street without rushing. Once out of sight of the boutique, I hurried to my car. I opened the driver's side door and slid in. April Mae was slumped down in the passenger seat.

"And?" I asked.

"I got it!" she screamed. April held the brooch aloft and then dropped it into my hand. "Are we a team or what?"

"We rock!" I shouted back.

"Let's get outta here before they come after us."

I put the car in gear and headed it toward home grinning like a dog with a brand new bone.

I spent the rest of the evening curled up with my pets and some popcorn, watching an old movie and admiring Grandma Tillie's brooch which I'd propped up on my bookshelf. I'd have to figure out a plan to keep it safely in my possession. Mel would not let this pass. If I knew anything, I knew that. For now, it was enough that I had it back.

Amidst my musings about keeping the family heirloom from being stolen again, I also mulled over the idea of April Mae and the gargantuan black Cadillac parked next door. Malone had seemed dead serious (pardon the expression) about the mob being active in Laguna Beach.

I yawned, and Dogbert and the two cats followed suit. Thelma and Louise both snuggled a little closer. I thanked my lucky stars that I dealt with the lighter side of life with people and their pets, and didn't see the seamier side Malone dealt with every day.

Sleep did not come easy. My mind raced like a hound on the hunt. The more I thought, the more I worried about April Mae and her dogged pursuit of finding information about her sister's killer.

CHAPTER SEVENTEEN

The next day Kitty's death was back in the news. I'd caught a teaser from morning anchor Maggie Rameriz about an update as I came in from a quick morning outing with Dogbert, but then they'd gone to break.

I waited, slipping off my shoes. Maybe there was a break in the case. The young anchor came back from commercial.

"We have some new developments in the murder of a Hollywood publicist. An unnamed source at Laguna Beach City Hall has leaked some information about the investigation, and now that leak is causing controversy. Police say speculation about the crime will cause unnecessary concern. And now let's talk to Dave McAndrews who is at the Laguna Beach Police Department."

They went to a live shot in front of the municipal complex which included City Hall, the police station, and the fire department. That explained where all the news vans had gone. I was happy for our neighborhood and sorry for Malone.

The live reporter continued, "Here the police work twenty-four/seven on the case following up on every possible lead, leaving nothing to chance, but they have no real suspects. The last thing they want is someone who they say is spouting off pure speculation or unsubstantiated rumors."

"What are those rumors?" the anchor asked from the newsroom. I was glad she'd asked. I wanted to know too.

"Our source tells us the police are following up on the idea the publicist's shooting might have been a mob hit."

"That is a surprise, Dave." The picture returned to the anchor in the studio. "Well, folks, we'll keep you informed as we learn more about this development."

As I turned off the TV and went to shower and get dressed for the day, I wondered if their source was the same "cousin of someone who works at the police department" as the guy April Mae had talked to at the gas station.

Later that evening, April Mae was seated on my patio while I watered the flower pots I'd lugged home from the Laguna Gardens Nursery. Chrysanthemums were great fall flowers in southern California, and the Santana yellows and Santana whites I'd picked up were already in full bloom.

April Mae wore a yellow top paired with orange and white flowered shorts. I don't mean this in a critical way, but she kind of looked like a lawn ornament in the midst of my colorful garden.

"Caro, I got a copy of Sissy's will in the mail today, and I hafta tell ya, you coulda knocked me over with a feather duster." She held up a thick stapled packet of legal-sized papers.

"The attorney told you the day of Kitty's funeral you were her main heir. What surprised you?"

"Well, first off. She left me her house and most all of her money. I don't know how much that is going to end up being but . . ." April Mae swallowed hard. "Caro, I've never had a house. I never thought I ever would." Big tears filled her eyes.

"Oh, sugar." I left my flower watering and went over to give her a squeeze. "Don't cry." I'd traded one kind of waterworks for another.

"I'm sorry. I just can't believe she would do that when she never even met me. I could be a no account loser for all she knew."

She was right. It was an incredible thing to do. "You know what? It is a big deal."

"The other part that surprised me was what she left to some other people."

"Really? Like who?"

"One of them is her business partner, Franklin Chesney. I can imagine she'd want to leave him something, but here's the crazy part. She left him a picture. Says he can pick it out."

"A what?"

"A picture. You know one of her pictures on the wall. Sissy sure had a lot of them."

"Then there's this woman, Tonya Miles. She also gets to pick out a picture and a pair of shoes."

"Shoes?" There had to be a story behind the footwear bequest.

"Yeah. Then the rest of her pictures she left to the Laguna Beach Art Museum. And the rest of everything else goes to me. Well, me and the cats."

"Wow." I'd thought it was nice Kitty had remembered her new found sister in her will, but she had more than remembered her.

"Look. I got this by mail." She tapped the papers. "A guy came to the door, and I had to sign for it. From the letter it looks like all the other people listed got a copy today too."

181

"Sounds reasonable, hon."

"I called up that lawyer guy and asked him if that meant I get the cats too. He said yes. So I have a house, and I have two cats. I tell you, I am in high cotton."

She looked like a kid at Christmas. A house and two cats. We should all be so happy to have those things.

"You are, sugar. You surely are." Yep, the woman had no idea.

"Tomorrow, I'm going to see Sissy's partner, Franklin, at their PR firm. I have some questions for him. Where is Century City?"

"Not far. Maybe an hour away, depending on traffic." Looks like I'd be calling first thing in the morning to see if I could reschedule my morning appointments. This was the kind of outing I was sure even Malone would agree I should not let April Mae go on alone.

We headed to Century City early before the traffic was too heavy, so it wasn't a bad drive. April Mae seemed a little overwhelmed by the congestion and by the impressive office building.

Franklin Chesney was with a client when we arrived at the Bardot and Chesney PR offices. In all the time I'd been neighbors with Kitty and had worked with Franklin and his Corgis as clients, I'd never been to their office. Franklin had a small apartment in Westwood. I'd always worked with his dogs there.

Space in this part of town was pricey. It confirmed what I'd thought — the firm had been doing well.

We checked in with the receptionist, Cherise, and then took a seat. Cherise, though not a young woman could have been a model herself. She seemed to be having a problem with an impatient client. When he turned, I recognized Clive, the grief-stricken artist from Kitty's funeral.

"I don't have all day to wait," he snapped at her.

"You didn't make an appointment," the receptionist said in a firm but pleasant voice.

Now why couldn't we find someone like her for our office?

It wasn't but a few minutes when she looked up and made eye-contact with us. "You can go in now."

We thanked her and stood. Clive had switched tactics, apparently realizing being a stinker was not very effective. He'd put away his petulant attitude and had now applied himself to charming Cherise.

Though full of himself, he truly was a

handsome guy. I hadn't realized it the night at the Pet Art Exhibition at Montage because his allergy symptoms had made him so miserable. Face it, a bright red nose isn't a great look for anyone.

His longish dark hair just brushed his shoulders, and his very vivid blue eyes (definitely contacts) set off his classic features. Super straight teeth made for a Hollywood smile. Though this was the first time I'd seen him smile. There was something dark and brooding about him, and I guessed it was a quality many women found attractive.

Cherise excused herself and ushered us down the hall to Franklin's office.

"Hello, Caro. So nice to see you." Franklin stood as we entered.

"Franklin, this is April Mae, Kitty's sister." I made the introductions, and he shook April's hand.

"The long lost sister, the one we didn't even know about. Please have a seat." He indicated the chairs in front of his desk and then dropped into his own. He still looked exhausted.

"How are you holding up?" I asked.

"Not too bad." Franklin moved some papers on his desk, but I'm not sure he even knew what he held.

"I think we met at the funeral, but I was pretty upset, and I don't much remember anybody I met." April, who'd been studying the floor, spoke softly. She'd been all confident bluster but now, faced with her sister's colleague, she seemed intimidated by Franklin and his formal manner.

"Kitty was not only my business partner, she was my best friend." Franklin looked directly at April Mae. He seemed a little confrontational. I wondered if he'd expected to inherit more than the bequest he'd been given.

"I got a copy of my Sissy's will in the mail and a letter from her lawyer. You're supposed to come by the house and pick out a picture." The pixie'd found her voice.

"Yes, I got a copy of Kitty's will, too. I have to say I was surprised." There it was again. That slight edge to his tone.

"I stopped in to find out when you'd like to come by."

"You could have just phoned."

"It seemed more personal to stop in." April Mae looked at me for confirmation. The excuse sounded lame even to me. In reality, we'd wanted to see his reaction and ask some questions.

"I see."

"You let me know when, just give me a

ring. You can come anytime, you hear." April Mae slid a paper with her phone number across the desk.

"Thank you." There was a sub-text to his words, but I couldn't figure out what it was. Was he irritated by April's down home expressions? Was he maybe just so busy that he was hoping we'd move on?

Franklin stood, dismissing us.

We remained seated. April shot me a wide-eyed look.

"There's one more thing," I said. Maybe more than one, but we'd start with this one. April Mae seemed to have lost her resolve again, so I stepped in.

"Yes?"

"The police came by and collected all of Kitty's mail. They say they have information she had received threats. Was that true? And do you know who was threatening her?" Okay, that was more than one.

"We had some threats." He sat back down.

"From whom?" I leaned forward.

"We weren't sure. There were four other publicists who had also received them. We'd notified the LAPD. The letters all came to the office. LAPD thought Russian mob. They'd invested in some film. Not our fault it went belly up, but some of our clients were involved."

"Do you think they could have made good on the threat and shot Kitty?" I had to ask the obvious question.

"Truthfully, no."

"Other theories, then?"

"If I were to worry about anybody, it would be Petra Rossi. She was furious with Kitty for dropping her. It got ugly." Franklin grimaced as if remembering the incident.

"Have you told the police?"

He looked up. Guilt washed over his face.

"I haven't," he admitted.

"Why would she be so angry?" Even I knew there were lots of other agencies to choose from. A fact I was sure was not lost on Franklin. Petra Rossi, a snowboarding superstar, could have her pick.

"She brought it on herself. Normally, once Kitty takes someone on as a client, she is loyal, even if they get themselves in a jam. Kitty works — worked —" he corrected himself. "Worked to mitigate the problem. You remember when Diana got arrested, and her publicist worked the press? Kitty was a master at turning around bad press."

"So what went wrong with Petra?"

"There were rumors Petra was pregnant. And she was. Then I guess she gave the baby up for adoption. She hid it all, lied to Kitty about the whole thing."

"Wow."

"Wow, is right." Franklin shook his head. "Now knowing more about Kitty's own background, I better understand why she was so adamant. The big thing was, she lied to us. That was the last straw. Kitty always said, we're on their side, but we have to be their best friend, their shadow, their Father confessor."

"Who is this Petra?" April asked.

"She's a big snowboarder from Alaska," I explained.

"We'd gotten her all kinds of great publicity. Product endorsements. Kitty was working on a movie deal for her when the rumors started."

"I guess I heard them, but there are always rumors, so I didn't put much stock in them." I didn't follow the tabloids.

"Sometimes they're based in fact." Franklin rubbed his hand over his bald head. "I was in New York working on a deal for another client when Kitty broke things off with her."

"She was upset about it?" I prompted.

"She came in the office a couple of weeks ago and was furious. Couldn't believe Kitty'd sent her a notice we were dropping her. That's the way it works with our contracts. Kitty always had a clause where we could drop someone with thirty days notice. And it worked the other way around too. They could fire us."

"Sorry to be so blunt, Franklin." I couldn't help but voice the thought. "But you're not the only game in town."

"No, but you know how it is in this business." He stood again. "You're dealing with major egos."

"Yeah, I'm sure that's true." It brought to mind Clive in the waiting area and his super-sized ego. He shouldn't have to wait. He was important. I guess in the star business you dealt with a lot of people who believe the world revolved around them.

"Thanks for your time, Franklin. We appreciate it." I shook his hand and held it for a minute. "You have to tell the police about Petra."

"I will." He patted my hand. Now that was more the Franklin I knew.

April held out her hand, but he didn't take it immediately. "Call me and let me know when you'd like to come by for your picture."

Much like Philippe, there was a visible wince. April seemed to have that effect.

"Have you thought any more about adopting?" I'd encouraged Franklin to consider getting another dog.

"I'm not ready."

"I understand." I took his arm as we walked out. "You think about it, though, okay?"

Clive was still in the waiting area, and it seemed he now had Cherise wrapped around his little finger.

He smiled and stood as we walked through, as if noticing us for the first time. What? Had we been invisible before?

"Hello, I'm Clive."

"Nice to meetcha, Clive. I'm April Mae but you can call me June."

The crazy moniker went right over Clive's head. Not about him, so not important.

"I hear you are Kitty Bardot's sister, and you have her painting cats. Are the cats painting again?" It wasn't quite a sneer but almost. I guess if you're allergic to cats, maybe you're not fond of the animals in general.

"Just a little," April Mae answered. "Getting their feet wet, so to speak." She giggled.

"Ridiculous," he pronounced. "Cats who paint. Dogs who paint. What will be next — chickens who paint?"

April Mae laughed at the idea.

I snickered, thinking about Diana's rooster, Walter.

I almost said, "Don't tempt this one. She's

an animal charmer; painting chickens just might be next." But I decided his question was rhetorical.

I also started to mention to Clive that we'd seen some of his work at the Arman gallery, but he'd already turned his back to us and resumed talking to Cherise.

When he wasn't looking, she gave us a wink. Clearly she was used to dealing with all the stars and wanna-be stars and their egos. Bardot and Chesney had a gem in her. We were having no luck in hiring someone for our office, and I was out of patience with Sourp . . . er . . . Sally Purser. See, I can get it right.

Maybe Cherise had a sister.

CHAPTER EIGHTEEN

I drove back to Laguna Beach with April Mae in pure chat mode. I'd taken PCH because we weren't in a big rush and put the convertible top down. What was the point of having one, if you didn't use it on a day like this one?

April Mae loved the sun, she loved the palm trees, she loved the wind blowing her hair all crazy. She reminded me of Dogbert with his ears flapping in the wind on a car ride. At any moment I expected her to hang her tongue out the window.

After what we'd learned from Franklin, it seemed clear there was at least a person of interest for the police to focus on. It made more sense than a mob hit. I couldn't picture Kitty in a *Get Shorty* scenario.

The drive went quickly, and we were home in no time. The sky was washed with primary blue, and there were a few clouds which brought to mind puffy peach pastries.

It was a picture-perfect day in Laguna Beach. I hoped the Chamber of Commerce had someone out taking photos. Even more, I hoped Walt was on the move today taking pictures. I stood a better chance of getting one of those.

I went by home so I could drop off April Mae and also let Dogbert out. While I was there I took the opportunity to call Malone and tell him about our talk with Franklin Chesney. I hoped Franklin would contact the police on his own about Petra Rossi, but I wasn't taking any chances.

My afternoon flew because it was filled with not only the appointments I had scheduled, but also the ones I'd moved from the morning.

I stopped by the office when I was finished to drop off paperwork on the clients I'd visited. Our unfriendly temp was busy on the phone, and I confess I slipped in quietly and back out just as silently because I just didn't want to deal with her grumpiness.

When we got together that evening April Mae was full of news. She'd tried to track down Petra Rossi but without any success. She'd done some reading about her on the Internet, and the snowboarder was also a crack shot. There were plenty of pictures of her posed not only with her snowboard but proudly holding various guns.

I'll admit it sounds far-fetched. It did seem, though, after Kitty dropped her, the girl's career had gone downhill. She'd had a driving while intoxicated arrest, broken up with the even-more-well-known-than-her snowboarder she'd been dating, and lost several of her product endorsement contracts. We didn't see anything about the movie deal Franklin had mentioned, but there was the possibility it hadn't panned out. She'd become a wild child. There were plenty of unflattering photos of her leaving hot-spots in LA, New York, and even one of a pub in London. It was a shame; she was a beautiful girl and an outstanding athlete to boot.

Maybe she'd blamed Kitty for her fall from grace and, fueled by anger and a penchant for alcohol, if the stories we read online were true, decided to go after the publicist who'd deserted her. What was it Franklin'd said? They had to be their client's best friend and their confessor. Maybe Petra felt her best friend had deserted her and had been bent on revenge.

Wonder where Petra Rossi had been the night of Kitty's murder? I know what you're thinking, but all I meant was that Malone should have no trouble finding out.

CHAPTER NINETEEN

April Mae had called Tonya Miles about coming to pick up her two bequests. A painting and a pair of shoes. We still hadn't discovered the story behind the shoes. But there just had to be one, didn't there?

She'd asked me to be present for moral support. I think the visit with Franklin had knocked a little of the glint off her rose-colored glasses.

Tonya arrived in style. Her Bentley was driven by a chauffeur who carefully parked the expensive car in April Mae's drive next to the Cadillac. There was a certain entertaining absurdity in the fancy-schmancy Bentley side-by-side with the pimpmobile. Or maybe I'm just easily amused.

The uniformed chauffeur held the door for Tonya and she stepped out. I felt sorry for the guy, long sleeves and a dark-colored cap in this sunshine.

I'd mostly seen the woman from a distance

in the past. Occasionally, I'd been outside when she'd picked up Kitty for a lunch or an evening engagement. The closest I'd been to her was the day of Kitty's funeral. She was small like April Mae and Kitty. But if Kitty Bardot had been solid gold, Tonya Miles was all brass.

Her imperious attitude was apparent, even from the front step where I stood waiting. She pointed at the backseat, and the chauffeur reached in the car and pulled out a Louis Vuitton bag containing a dog. Oops, two dogs. Two very small dogs. She held her arms out for the bag, and he handed it over.

Now, the Louis Vuitton brand has been around since 1854, and the distinct LV label marks all of their products. They make a ton of different types of trunks, totes, and purses and have quite the celebrity following, but I don't think Mr. Vuitton ever imagined his luxury bags being used as doggie carriers.

I held open the front door so Tonya could enter, and a waft of expensive perfume engulfed me as she stepped through. Once in, she handed me the bag of dogs.

"I understand you're a professional pet therapist. Please keep Spike and Hulk feeling safe. Kitty's monstrous cats could literally eat them in one bite."

It was an exaggeration, but they were tiny compared to Tobey and Minou, who'd come from their cat perches to see what all the commotion was about. Spike and Hulk peeked out the top of the bag.

Tonya kissed each glistening nose. "Poor sweeties, you must be terrified."

In my professional pet therapist opinion, they didn't look terrified. They looked ridiculous. The miniature teacup Malti-Poo puppies were dressed in matching smoking jackets ala Hugh Hefner. They were adorable dogs, but they did not appear happy about the wardrobe choice.

Tonya suddenly noticed April Mae standing there. "I suppose you're the sister." She looked down her surgically perfect nose at her.

The little sprite had dressed for the occasion with her new black Laguna Beach tank top and a purple mini-skirt she must have had since high school. "The closet is this way. In the bedroom."

"I know where the closet is." Tonya's haughty tone seemed unnecessary.

She strutted her stuff down the hall to Kitty's bedroom. She paused for a moment at one doorway, stepped inside Kitty's study, and pointed to a small painting. "I'll take that one."

She then continued on to the master bedroom and Kitty's still very organized closet.

Wow, the woman came in first for Most Rude. April Mae and I exchanged a look, but kept our thoughts to ourselves.

Tonya brought the makeup stool from Kitty's bedroom into the closet and proceeded to try on nearly every pair of shoes on the shelves.

She'd pull out one pair and then the next, trying each on in turn and then discarding them for another. These were very, very nice shoes: black Christian Louboutin pumps, brocade Fendi flats, Gucci evening shoes in metallic python, two-toned Michael Kors sandals in red with a high spiky silver heel and lime patent-leather Kate Spade loafers. I wondered exactly what criteria she would eventually use to decide on which shoes to take.

At one point she slipped on a pair of blue suede Via Spiga pumps and then pulled something out of the toe. A brilliant ring glittered in her hand.

She handed it to April Mae. "Here, you'd better put this somewhere else."

"You might want to lock it up in Kitty's safe," I advised.

"Oh, don't bother." Tonya waved her hand dismissively. "It's paste."

"What?" April Mae and I both asked in tandem.

"Fake, you ninnies." She laughed as she reached for yet another pair of shoes, but it wasn't a pleasant laugh. It was just an older version of the Mean-Girl snicker. "It's phony. Not real diamonds. Nice looking piece but about as real as my hair color."

I guessed more than her hair color wasn't real, but there didn't seem to be anything gained from going there.

April Mae handed me the ring. I turned it over in my hand. It was a great fake. It had fooled me, and I had an eye for good jewelry. A plan began to form in my mind.

"Who does fakes this good?" I asked Tonya.

"I have all my expensive pieces duplicated by Selma. An exclusive jeweler in the Valley." Tonya had worked her way through half of the closet.

"Are you working with the police?" She turned and pointed her false-eye-lashed gaze at me.

"I am not working with anyone," I answered in my no-nonsense, heel-you-bad-dog voice. "I'm simply here to support April Mae."

Tonya reached out for the designer dogs I still held and rubbed each tiny head in turn with one French-manicured finger.

"You," Tonya turned her fancy finger on me, "should make sure the police know about Franklin Chesney and his secret life. The last time Kitty and I had lunch, they had a major tiff. She'd asked him to cover some unimportant party so she could come to a party at my house. He said he couldn't, he was going out of town. Kitty said, and I quote, 'I am sick of you and your secret life. Maybe you need to think about whether you really want to stay in the business or not.' She was very upset with him."

She suddenly noticed her finger, still raised in the air. "Oh hell, I hope I haven't chipped a nail. These take forever to be repaired. The flecks are actual twenty-four-karat gold." She held her hands out for April Mae and me to admire.

"What is Franklin's secret life?" If we had to put up with the pretentious attitude, at least maybe we could get some real information out of the deal.

"I have no idea, but now I hear she left him no money. Before you came onto the scene . . ." This time she poked the gold-flecked finger at April Mae. "He was to inherit everything. Well, except for the part she'd set aside to take care of her precious kitties. I see in my copy of the will she didn't change that provision." She stood and walked out of the closet carrying a pair of Stuart Weitzman special edition pumps.

I still had no idea how she'd decided.

She'd left the rest of the shoes in a pile on the floor for us to pick up, like we were shoe department staff at Neiman Marcus. And I tell you, I've never done anything that rude to a salesperson. Though I'll bet Tonya has.

Tonya held her arms open for the bag containing the teacup pups, and I reluctantly handed it over. They were adorable and I was sure well cared for. But brocade smoking jackets? Poor puppies.

She shifted the shoes so she could carry the puppy bag. "I'll have Theo come back in for the painting. I hope you have something to wrap it."

Then she was off. Out the door.

No nice-to-meet-you. No thank-you. No good-bye.

Geez Louise, the woman was a piece of work.

Theo, in his stiff long-sleeved uniform, soon appeared at the door. April Mae had let him in while I'd looked around Kitty's office for something to wrap the painting in. Finally locating some gift wrap and tissue paper, I swaddled the small piece of art, a Jackson Pollock if I wasn't mistaken. Theo took it from me, thanked us, and wasted no time getting back to his employer.

I pitied him almost as much as I did the poor pups.

Grandma Tillie used to say, "A high-steppin' horse is a bumpy ride." Tonya Miles was the personification of that old adage.

The next evening Franklin Chesney arrived to collect his piece of art. It seemed odd to see him in jeans. Even when I'd worked with his Corgis at his apartment, the man was always in office clothes. Today he sported jeans — granted they were nice jeans — and a polo shirt. Also not tacky, evidenced by the little Ralph Lauren logo on the front.

In spite of our rocky week, April Mae had asked me to be present again. I justified it that it fell under keeping her safe and keeping an eye on her.

Unlike Tonya Miles, Franklin knew exactly what he was after. He politely engaged in a little small talk, then pointed out which of the paintings he wanted and wrapped it in the paper he'd brought along.

Unlike the piece Tonya Miles had selected, I didn't recognize the artist. The painting was a soft pastoral scene with a rustic barn in the background and a group of goats in the foreground. It was an unexpected choice as far as I was concerned, but he picked it without hesitation.

April Mae offered him something to drink, but he declined. I attempted to engage him in conversation, which I hoped would zip right to a possible secret life discussion.

"Tonya Miles was here yesterday to pick up her bequest. She chose a small Pollack I hadn't even realized Kitty owned and a pair of Stuart Weitzman pumps probably worth nearly as much as the painting."

"Sounds like Tonya." Franklin stood near the door clearly ready to be on his way.

"She doesn't seem like Kitty's type." An unlikely friendship if I ever saw one.

"Oh, Tonya provided Kitty entrée into all the best parties."

"And what did Kitty provide Tonya?"

Franklin actually chuckled at my observation. "Well," he said. "I always believed Kitty had something on Tonya. The only explanation I could come up with. Tonya Miles doesn't give favors easily."

"I can imagine." I thought of the woman and her attitude yesterday. "I don't get the shoes and a painting. There must be a story to go with that bequest."

"Whatever it was, Tonya may be the only one who knows. Otherwise, Kitty took her reasons to her grave."

"Kitty's will and its details seem to have been a surprise to the beneficiaries," I noted.

"Yeah, all three of us."

"Five, if you count the cats," April Mae added.

"Listen," Franklin sighed and set his painting on the floor. "Let me make this easy for you. If you're wondering whether I'm upset at not being left more of Kitty's estate, I'm not."

"You sure can't be happy about being cut-off like a red-headed stepchild." April Mae finally found her voice. Accent and all.

"I'm not exactly 'cut-off' as you put it, dear."

"How so?" I asked.

"When Kitty made me a partner three years ago, we bought survivors insurance for the business. That way, if either one of us died, the other had insurance to cover the loss. We saw our partnership as very even. So we covered each other."

"Oh." Then it seemed like it wasn't a case of him thinking he was to get a big inheritance, but he had still profited from Kitty's death.

"Satisfied?" His face was red all the way

to the top of his bald head. He picked the painting back up.

"Yes." April Mae and I both bobbed our heads.

"I cared for Kitty as a person. As a friend." His voiced tightened with emotion. "Which is more than I can say for some of her other so-called friends. Maybe Ms-Botoxed-Bouffant-Big-Shot didn't want whatever Kitty knew about her to get out. Appearances are all Tonya Miles cares about." His voice broke on the words. Franklin took his art and left.

Wow. I wondered at the show of emotion.

I also wondered how he'd managed to use all those "B" words to describe Tonya Miles without giving in to the obvious one.

After Franklin's outburst, I couldn't help but think we'd let Tonya Miles off the hook too easily. No doubt the killer instinct lived in her, but nasty words seemed to be her weapon of choice. I couldn't see her firing a gun; she might chip a nail. Still, April Mae and I had both been so taken aback by her sheer insolence, we'd not really asked the questions we'd intended.

We were no closer to knowing what secret life Franklin Chesney was hiding. It was clear we needed to talk to Tonya Miles again, and finding out where she lived was as easy as putting her name in Google.

The woman showed up on every celebrity stalker site there was. Maybe the economy was in a slump, but you sure couldn't tell it by the money being spent on Hollywood parties.

Pool parties, yacht parties, beach parties. The diamonds sparkled, the champagne flowed, and the paparazzi snapped pictures.

We finally tore ourselves from the computer where we'd been sucked into looking at cute pictures of celebrities' pets. (Did you know Justin Bieber had a pet snake named Johnson, and George Clooney, a potbellied pig, Max?)

Back on task, it wasn't long before we had Tonya's address and a plan.

CHAPTER TWENTY

We drove to Tonya Miles' estate in Bel Aire without any problem.

With any luck we'd leave with clearer information on Franklin or at least a direction to research. And just maybe, we'd get the goods on Tonya.

But things did not go according to plan.

I know. I know. When do they ever?

No sooner had we arrived than the silver Bentley pulled out from the estate and onto Bellagio. We had to decide quickly whether to follow the car or stick with our original plan.

Seeing the fortified entrance between us and the Miles estate, we did a U-turn and followed the Bentley. If Tonya was on a shopping spree and headed for Beverly Hills, it would be easier to accost her on Rodeo Drive than get past that big gate.

The Bentley rolled onto Sunset Boulevard toward downtown. Darn. Looked like we weren't going shopping after all.

As the driver headed deeper into the fashion district, we almost lost them a couple of times.

At first I thought the destination was Santee Alley, a well-known spot for designer knock-offs. But the car went past the popular Fashion District and into a warehouse area. Not many Bentleys here.

When the car glided to a stop, the driver got out and opened the rear passenger door.

A small woman wearing a baggy denim housedress and clunky plastic shoes stepped to the curb. Her head was covered by a huge ugly scarf, and spongy pink hair curlers poked out the front and sides. The scarf was so big it dwarfed her.

Shoot. We'd followed Tonya's housekeeper or some other member of her staff who she must have sent on an errand. Or maybe she'd loaned the car and driver to a valued staff member.

Though the kindness angle didn't seem to fit what I knew of Tonya Miles so far. In fact, from what we'd seen, Mr. Ebenezer Scrooge had nothing on her.

"That's not her," April Mae said. "What do we do?"

"If it's someone who works for her, maybe

we can glean some info from them," I suggested.

"We've come this far. I'm game."

We parked the car down the block.

The housekeeper shuffled into one of the alleys. There was a white older model van parked against the building.

Suddenly this didn't seem like such an adventure. I hoped we hadn't wandered into a drug deal.

As I looked closer, I could see it wasn't a drug deal we'd wandered into, but a faux fashion extravaganza. The back of the van was open and filled to the roof with designer purses: Louis Vuitton, Prada, Chanel, Coach, even Hermes.

"Whatcha lookin' for, girls?" One of the guys, a muscular gent in shorts and work boots, who didn't exactly fit my idea of a fashion consultant, had come up behind us.

"Not sure yet. What've you got?" I answered evenly.

"Play along." I whispered under my breath to April Mae.

"Cool." She grinned. "We're undercover again."

We closed in on Tonya's housekeeper, just as she reached for a very authentic-looking Chanel knock-off. Her arm slipped out from the shawl, and she picked up the distinctive black quilted bag.

As she did, I noticed her fingernails. A special French-manicure with little flecks of gold. I'd bet my Miss Texas crown, those flecks were "real twenty-four-karat gold."

Holy Prada, Batman!

This wasn't some Miles family house staff on an errand. This was Ms. High and Mighty Tonya Miles herself. I latched onto her skinny wrist before she could get away.

"We need to talk."

She turned and looked me in the face. "Let go of me, or you'll be sorry."

"I'm already sorry. So, this is what Kitty had on you. Did you kill her because she was going to out you?"

"Hardly." She bit out the words like she was chewing nails. "We had a mutually beneficial relationship. She kept me in designer clothes with her cast-offs. I kept her on the A-list for the best parties. Now, without her as my supplier, I'm reduced to this."

Geez Louise, woman, would you like some cheese with that whine?

Suddenly our theory that Kitty had been blackmailing Tonya didn't seem so plausible.

"Get away from me before someone recognizes me." She reached up with her free hand and pulled the ugly scarf closer around

210

her face. "I'm telling you, Franklin is the only one who stood to gain from Kitty's death. You check on what you don't know about him. I guarantee it's something bigger than handbag knock-offs."

I dropped her wrist. If she was bluffing, she was one heck of a bluffer.

April Mae had only at that moment realized I wasn't man-handling Tonya's housekeeper but Tonya herself and began to sputter.

"She's, she's —" April Mae pointed at the disguised socialite.

"Come on. Let's get out of here." I grabbed April's arm, and we raced back to the Mercedes.

Our foray into stalking had been a dud. Surprising, but still a dud.

I wondered how the heck we were going to explain this one to Malone. I was about to find out, because no sooner were we back in town, than the detective called. I let it go to voicemail, not ready to explain how following someone who may (or may not) be a suspect does not qualify as meddling in his investigation.

Malone asked me to coffee the next morning to discuss the case.

Yes, you heard that right.

211

I couldn't believe it either when I listened to the message he'd left, asking me to meet him at the Koffee Klatch at eight.

I waited in line for Verdi to finish up with the customer in front of me. As usual, she handled the early morning crush with aplomb.

"Any luck on a new job?" I asked as I handed over my payment.

"I've had a couple of interviews, but so far no luck."

"You can feel free to put me down as a reference if you think it might help." I fished one of my cards from my bag and handed it to her. I felt for the girl. She'd been holding down two jobs for who knows how long, and I guessed probably didn't have a lot of money put away for a safety net.

"Thanks, Caro." She took the card. "I really appreciate it."

I moved so the person behind me could step up to the register.

"Coffee black." It was Malone. None of those frou-frou drinks for him.

I hadn't heard him approach, but like you've probably noticed, he's mostly the strong and silent type. That's why the invitation to talk about Kitty's murder was so unexpected. Granted, I was supposed to be keeping an eye on April Mae, but I'd been reporting in by phone.

I found an empty table outside in the shade. It was early enough that most of the tables were free and clean. I'd picked a Caroline Rose long denim blouse and black skinny pants. Not that I'd dressed up for Malone, or for that matter not that he'd notice if I had.

The detective soon followed and slouched into the chair opposite mine.

"So, Caro, saving the world one coffee barista at time?" He lifted his cup and took a sip.

"What?"

"The girl at the counter with the burgundy hair."

"Oh, poor kid, she's lost her other job. You don't have any openings at the police department, do you? She's a phenomenal multi-tasker."

"No, no openings for multi-taskers right now."

"Well, if you hear of anything . . ."

"I'll be sure to let you know."

"Thanks." I tasted my hazelnut latte; it was delicious. Verdi had made the drinks, and hers were always better.

Since I had Malone's attention, I took the opportunity to ask him who at the PD would be a person to talk to if I thought someone was in an abusive relationship. I was determined to help Diana's next door neighbor if I could.

He gave me the name of their domestic abuse counselor and said he'd let her know I'd be calling.

Malone placed his coffee on the table and leaned forward. "Tell me what you've found out about Franklin Chesney, Kitty's partner."

Ah, so that's what this was about. The police were zeroing in on someone, and that someone must be Franklin.

I brain-dumped everything we'd learned.

Malone didn't take notes, but then he never did. He was attentive, I'll give him that, but memory can be faulty, and I wished he'd write down a few of the details.

"Will you be talking to Franklin again soon?"

"April Mae and I have to go back to his office to find out about how Kitty handled the cats as clients, since they're painting again."

Malone's reaction was similar to what Walt's had been. I gathered he wasn't going to be in the market for a Tobey and Minou painting to hang in his office.

"Let me know if Franklin Chesney lets slip anything about this 'secret life' Tonya

Miles believes he has." Malone took a last sip of his coffee and stood to leave.

"You got it. I'd better be going too." I also got to my feet. "We have a temp working reception at the office, and you never know what the day is going to bring. This latest one, well, let me put it this way, she is not a multi-tasker."

As I said the words, I realized the answer, to both Verdi's problem and mine, had been right in front of me all along.

Isn't that the way it often is — sometimes you're too close to see the solution?

We said good-bye, and Malone disappeared as quickly as he'd appeared.

I headed back into the Koffee Klatch to discuss the idea with Verdi. Then I was off to talk to my office mates about a burgundy-haired multi-tasker who was about to make all of our lives so much easier.

CHAPTER TWENTY-ONE

The next day, April Mae and I were back to the offices of Bardot and Chesney. I'd insisted on driving partly because I couldn't get past the idea of the possibility the Cadillac, as much as April Mae loved it, probably had a former life as a mob car. The other part of the equation was that it was one thing for April Mae to tool around Laguna Beach, but LA driving was a whole other story. I mean, she had to sit on pillows to drive the darn thing.

We'd made an appointment to see Franklin, and I was glad he'd been able to work us in.

This time there were a couple of people in the waiting room. One was a young woman with a striking resemblance to a young Elizabeth Taylor. The dark wavy hair, the violet eyes, and the curves. An older woman was with her. One could only assume maybe her mother or a relative of some sort.

We let Cherise know we'd arrived, albeit a little early. I'd overestimated the drive time as traffic had been, for once, under control. Still I was glad I had; you never knew when the 405 would suddenly become a parking lot. Paralyzed over an accident or construction.

"Ms. Ciccone, Mr. Chesney will see you now."

The young woman startled a bit and then stood. She'd been lost in admiring her reflection in the mirrored tiles across the room.

Okay, so maybe it wasn't just Clive. Perhaps a bit of narcissistic personality disorder was a requirement in the star business. I'd seen my share of it in the pageant circuit. Not every contestant, but there had been a ton of big egos. Maybe in Hollywood you needed a super-sized ego to survive. Still, I'd met some genuinely nice people like Diana Knight and Kitty Bardot.

Violet-Eyes was in Franklin's office no more than fifteen to twenty minutes when she came back out with some papers in hand.

She thanked Cherise, and then she and the older woman left.

"He's ready for you now." Cherise must have received some sort of signal from

Franklin.

When we stepped into his office, I was again struck by how harried he seemed. If he had any hair on his head, I had the sense he'd have been pulling it out. And, since Kitty's death, the man appeared to have aged ten years at least.

"Beautiful girl," I noted.

"What?" Franklin looked up from the papers he perused.

"The girl who just left. She's quite beautiful," I repeated. "Is she talented, as well?"

"She will be when Kimberly and Saul are done with her."

"Acting coaches?"

"Voice coaches. The girl is a natural as far as the acting goes, but her accent is atrocious." He looked at April by my side and suddenly realized what he'd said. "Nothing against accents." He attempted a recovery.

"No insult taken at all, sweetie." He couldn't know it, but April Mae really wasn't insulted.

"What can I do for you ladies?"

"April Mae wanted to talk to you about Tobey and Minou."

"What about them?"

"Kitty had represented the cats herself as their publicist, and now that they're painting again, I wondered if you'd want to represent them." If he could resist that hopeful voice, he was one hard-hearted guy.

"I hadn't realized they were painting again."

"They are," she giggled. "I've been workin' with them every day lately. We're taking their newest pictures to Philippe Arman on Friday. They done real great work, and he's arranging a show."

"Of course, I'll represent them. It's the least I can do for Kitty."

"Thanks! That's so nice." April Mae stood up, clearly glad to have that part out of the way.

"Cherise will send you some papers so it's all official."

I rose also. "I guess you handle a variety of clients. I knew Kitty handled models, actors, and some sports figures, but I didn't realize until we saw Clive the last time we were here that you handled artists as well."

"Clive who? We don't, I mean *I* don't," Franklin stumbled. "Sorry. I can't seem to get used to the idea that there's no 'we' anymore."

"But that guy, the not-so-tall, but dark and handsome artist. He was here the last time we were here and also at Kitty's funeral."

"Oh, that guy. He'd come in to try to talk

me into taking him on. Kitty'd already turned him down."

"Oh, I assumed he was a client."

"No, he isn't. And he isn't going to be." His tone said he was done discussing it. He stood and walked us to the door. "I'll have Cherise send you the papers. I look forward to working with the cats. And you."

Franklin's slight hesitation and his pained expression said he wasn't all that happy to be working with April Mae. Maybe the guy needed to work with a voice coach himself to see if he could eliminate the condescending tone.

"Thanks for your time, Franklin." I shook Franklin's hand.

"Yeah, thanks." April Mae, never content with a handshake, hugged him good-bye.

As we left, we stopped for a quick chat with Cherise under the guise of making sure she had April Mae's contact information. She confirmed Franklin disappeared from time and time, but either she didn't know where he went, or the woman was doing her best to keep his confidence. An admirable quality. Unless he was a murderer.

On the way back to the car April Mae and I talked about Franklin. I still didn't see him as a cold-blooded assassin, and shooting a person down the way Kitty had been would take a heartless killer. Maybe he'd arranged a contract killing. If the mob hit was really a possibility, it could be as simple as he was involved somehow with them. I thought back over what we'd learned. Franklin knew where Kitty was going to be the night she died. His whereabouts were unaccounted for as far as we knew.

He did have a motive, if cash was what was he'd needed. However, my sense was that Kitty had been even more valuable to the agency, and to Franklin, alive than any amount of survivor's payout.

The conclusion we came to? We needed to follow him.

We waited in the street with the car running, and it wasn't long before Franklin's black Lexus drove through the parking garage exit. I pulled in behind him. This would be wasted surveillance if he was only headed toward his apartment.

He turned north on Galaxy Way and then onto Avenue of the Stars. It was early in the day, but traffic was still brisk as Franklin pulled into a parking lot. He got out of the Lexus and changed vehicles.

The new hottest publicist to the stars now drove a late model red Chevy Silverado truck. He'd also replaced his suit with jeans before he'd left the office.

Following him through traffic, he merged onto the 405, and we were right behind. While the Lexus had been harder to follow, the red truck was much easier. We managed to keep the pickup in sight, and he continued north. April Mae did a great job keeping him in view. I apparently didn't do as good following without being seen, because as the truck pulled off the freeway, he turned into a parking lot, rolled to a stop and waved us forward.

Franklin got out of the truck and walked to my car. He didn't look too happy.

"I can save you two some trouble," he said. "I'm headed to Agua Dulce. It's a long trip, so you may want to gas up."

"Agua Dulce?" The only thing I knew about the place was the nearby Vasquez Rocks Natural Area Park, which was a popular Hollywood filming location. "Why are you going to Aqua Dulce?"

"Well, not that it's any of your business, but I have a ranch there."

"A ranch?"

"Yes, a goat ranch."

"You raise goats?" I suddenly noticed the vanity plate on the red pickup said, "GOATZ."

"I raise Myotonic goats."

I knew nothing about goats. We'd had a few goats on the family ranch in Texas, but mostly we had cattle. Goats are generally cute. Nothing sensational about them. Not exactly a deep dark secret.

April Mae leaned forward to look at him. "Your secret is that you raise goats?"

"Yes, Myotonic goats. Some people call them fainting goats."

"Oh, I've seen those kind. They are so adorable! Does it hurt them when they fall?"

"Why would you need to keep goat farming a secret?"

April Mae and I spoke at once.

Franklin looked off in the distance, like he wished we'd disappear, but then apparently decided to answer.

"Kitty herself had suggested I not talk about it. We're very much seen as an extension of our clients. That's why it was so important for her to go to all the best parties. Which is why she maintained her relationship with that beast of a woman, Tonya Miles."

Fainting goats? Really? I felt silly.

I also had a great idea about a dog for Franklin. I'd found a new home for Rawnsley, the Great Pyrenees at the animal shelter. Oh, and I had a thought about Diana's goat, Henny, who Bella had thought was sickly.

Turns out if you have the facts, it helps solve a lot of things.

Like the pastoral painting he'd chosen from Kitty's collection. The one with the rustic barn and the goats.

We apologized to Franklin for thinking he was part of the mob, part of some secret scandal, part of a plot to kill his partner.

Actually we didn't apologize for any of those theories. We kept all those to ourselves and simply apologized for following him.

I gave him Don Furry's number to contact about potentially adopting Rawnsley, and we wished him a wonderful goat-herding weekend.

By the way, he says the goats don't actually faint; their muscles stiffen and they appear to faint. He also assured April Mae they don't feel any pain when it happens.

Franklin headed on north to his goat ranch, and we headed back south toward Laguna Beach.

CHAPTER TWENTY-TWO

After our two ill-fated forays into following people, I was more than ready to leave the shadowing of suspects to the police. The next day began with what had become the usual, a news story about Kitty's death.

The irony was not lost on me that Kitty, whose job had been getting her clients in the news, would not have been thrilled with the publicity. For one thing, they continued to use the same tired photo of Kitty at a premier from a couple of years ago. There was a new angle today, but still the same picture of Kitty entering Grauman's Chinese Theater.

The voice-over was full of melodrama, "This has all the making of a Hollywood murder mystery, but investigators seem to have little evidence to go on. They have looked at footage from red light cameras, private security cameras, literally hundreds of hours of footage. Forensic experts we spoke to tell us it sounds like it was personal, but was it road rage, a crime of passion, or some manner of revenge?"

They switched to a view of the footage from the night of Kitty's death. "According to the Laguna Beach Police Department, the first 911 call they received simply said that a car had crashed into a light pole. Now, more than two weeks since that call, police seem no closer to solving this crime."

The shot went back to the studio, and the veteran anchor chimed in, "The death of Kitty Bardot, whose hard-hitting style was contrasted by her petite blonde looks and quick smile, has hit Hollywood hard, maybe because it always seemed like she was everywhere. She attended almost every premiere, party, or awards event. Unmarried and with no children, Ms. Bardot focused all of her attention on her clients and her two cats. Now Hollywood has stepped up for Kitty Bardot. Yesterday, Franklin Chesney, her partner in the PR firm they ran, announced a fund has been put together by several of her clients and friends offering a ten-thousand dollar reward for information leading to the arrest of her killer."

Wowza. That amount, though pocket change to many of Kitty's crowd, was nothing to shake a stick at, and would undoubtedly bring the crazies out of the woodwork. I'd bet the phones were ringing (and Lorraine was swearing) at the Laguna Beach police station right now. I could only imagine what Detective Malone had to say about the reward.

I showered and dressed quickly. I'd run a little behind because I'd gotten caught up in the news story.

I had a meeting at nine with the other business owners in my shared office about hiring Verdi. Then Grandma Tillie's brooch and I were going to visit Selma, the jeweler who Tonya Miles had sworn was a master at producing reproductions.

The meeting with my office mates — the accountant, the real estate agent, and the psychic — went well. I know, it sounds like the beginning to a bad joke, doesn't it? I still felt like the psychic owed us an explanation of why she hadn't been able to forewarn us about Paris, our former receptionist, leaving or our miserable matches with unsuitable temps. What good was it if we couldn't rely on each other for shared services?

No matter, they were all in agreement we would give Verdi a try, based on my recommendation. I had no doubt she would win them over on her own merit.

I hurried to my car, called Verdi and gave her the good news. She was to start the next day. Then checked my directions and headed to the Valley to meet with the jeweler.

I'd called Malone with my report on Franklin and his goat-raising secret. I wished I'd been able to make my report in person so I could have seen his face. But I have to tell you I could hear him tapping his pencil on his desk while we talked. I couldn't see his irritated expression, but I could picture it.

It goes without saying, he was not thrilled we'd followed Franklin.

"Did you ever find out anything regarding the client who was so upset, Petra Rossi?" I asked.

"We checked her out." He hesitated and then went on. I think he was afraid we might tail her. "Believe it or not, she was the special guest at a charity fund-raiser in New York on the night Kitty Bardot was murdered."

"Well, shoot." I sighed. "Where does that leave us?"

"It leaves you nowhere." I think I heard his pencil snap. "You are not to investigate. You are not to follow suspects. You are simply to keep an eye on April Mae Wooben and keep her out of trouble."

Sam had dinner planned at the Balboa Bay Club in Newport Beach, and I'd been looking forward to it. We'd been cheated out of a leisurely dinner the day I'd found the gun in April's truck, and we'd finally been able to reschedule.

The First Cabin restaurant always kind of reminds me a bit of a cruise liner, and I think that's their intent. The big windows look out on sailboats and the Pacific coastline, and the food is outstanding.

I'd picked a sleeveless sheath in bold blue and white by Maranda, a new LA designer. I loved her combination of the traditional with a twist. Old-fashioned but flirty, it was a fun, feel-good, pick.

Once we were seated, Sam asked me about the investigation and what had been going on with April Mae and if she'd forgiven me.

We ordered, and then I filled him in. I realized as we talked that a lot had happened over the past few days.

He enjoyed the story about following Tonya Miles, though his face did get a little serious when I talked about shadowing her through downtown LA and into an alley. But when I told him about Franklin and our discovery of his secret life as a goat farmer, I thought Sam would shoot his elegant "Belle Cote" Chardonnay right out his nose. Not that he ever would, you understand, but it was a hoot to see him try not to in the midst of the uber-exclusive club with its hovering staff.

"Good grief, Caro! How did you maintain after that revelation?" he'd finally recovered enough to ask.

"I'm not sure." I laughed, picturing April Mae and I hot on the trail of Franklin in his red Silverado. What the man must have thought when he saw us behind him.

"What next?" he asked as our entrees arrived.

"That's just it, Sam." I took a sip of the lively and exotic wine. "I'm afraid we're at a dead-end. Petra Rossi has an air-tight alibi, Tonya Miles really doesn't have a motive, and Franklin's secret life turned out to be a fainting goat farm. Crazy as it sounds, I guess we're back to a mob hit."

"What do the police say?"

"I talked to Detective Malone earlier today, but he didn't give out any details." I took a bite of my salmon.

"I know you can't leave this alone, but please promise me you'll not take unnecessary chances that put you in danger."

I started to poo-poo his concern, but the unusually serious look on his face stopped me.

He reached across the table and took my hand. "Caro, I know you don't need my help, but if things get out of control, give me your word that you'll call me?"

"I promise, Sam."

He sat quietly for a few minutes studying my face.

I studied him back, not an onerous assignment at all.

Finally, I broke the silence. "I'm not really investigating, though, so I'm not in any danger. I'm simply keeping an eye on April Mae."

"I know." He let go of my hand, and we went back to our food. "But I worry."

On the drive back to Laguna Beach, I filled Sam in on the situation with our office receptionist leaving, bringing Verdi from the Koffee Klatch to replace our grouchy temporary worker and other more mundane things.

When he kissed me good-night, Sam reiterated his concern. "I am going out of town for a few days, but promise me you'll call if you need anything. I can have our security people at your disposal in minutes."

"No need to worry," I assured him. "I'm sure April Mae and I are in no danger."

CHAPTER TWENTY-THREE

I have to say though I'd been skeptical about the idea of dogs and cats painting, there was something appealing about Tobey and Minou's new art. April Mae had chosen a mixture of soft blues and vivid red-orange hues. Maybe it was just that the colors in the new art spoke to me in the same sense Laguna Beach did. Whatever the reason, the paintings were fun.

I'd helped April Mae wrap the canvases to protect them, and we'd loaded them into her car.

While I always felt a little freaky about riding in the mob car, in this case we needed the extra space because the paintings were so big. They never would have fit in my roadster even with the convertible top down.

The idea of Philippe Arman doing a whole month long exhibition of cat art still made me shake my head. Internally, that is. I would have never told April Mae to her face

I wasn't completely sure the cats were artists.

And I certainly would have never told her I wasn't even convinced Philippe Arman thought so either. That's not to say the man didn't know his art. I'm sure he did. He also knew his business, and his business was selling art.

In the past several months, there'd been a huge interest in both canine and feline paintings. Serious art collectors were decrying it a hoax, but art collectors around the globe with an appreciation for satire were buying up the pet art like mad. Which, of course, in turn drove up prices. I'm sure a concept not lost on Philippe.

He was calling this exhibition, *Mewsings.* I hoped Diana was back from Italy in time for the event. It was right up her alley.

Once we'd carefully loaded the Caddy, we went back in for our handbags, then headed to the Arman Gallery.

Dusk had settled for the day and rewarded us with one of those priceless Pacific sunsets that are one of the reasons real estate with a view in Laguna Beach brings such a premium price.

The deeper orange where sky met water said it would be dark soon. Lordy, I loved Laguna Beach sunsets. I wondered if Tobey and Minou would paint one for me.

Artistic cats, a car from the mob, and a long-lost sister. Plus a will detailing the distribution of millions of dollars, two paintings, and a pair of designer shoes. The world had gone bonkers.

I leaned back in the leather seat with a sigh. I cared about April Mae, I really did, but some days I felt like ever since she'd shown up next door, my life had become a cartoon episode. Most days, I wasn't sure if I was Wile E. Coyote or the Roadrunner.

Maybe it was because I was so lost in my thoughts that I didn't react right away to the sound of something hitting the side of the car.

At first, I thought fireworks. Then I thought rocks. It was like I couldn't put the two sensations together.

Something made a loud crack.

Something hit the side of the car again.

Several somethings in a row. Too hard and too close together to be rocks unless they were being thrown by a whole crowd of major league pitchers.

April slammed on the brakes and started to get out. I grabbed her arm. "Wait!"

I don't know if I was channeling Wile E. Coyote or what, but something told me this was not going to turn out well.

The sounds stopped.

We heard the squeal of tires. After a few minutes of silence, I jumped out. Too late to see the make or model of the car. It was long gone. A license plate number was never a possibility.

April was also out of the car. "Could you see anything?"

"No, not enough light. I think the car was silver or gray, but I'm not even sure about that."

"Caro, look at this." Her voice was suddenly tense with emotion.

I walked around to her side of the car.

You know those cartoons where bullets bounce off of cars? Yeah, not in real life. There were at least a dozen puncture holes in the side of the Caddy.

I didn't know how it was possible we'd not been hit.

I didn't know how it was possible we were not dead.

Response times are great in Laguna Beach. A police cruiser, lights flashing, arrived in under three minutes. Detective Malone arrived two minutes later.

Malone asked us to wait in the back of the cruiser. Second time in a police cruiser. It was still creepy.

For a while April Mae and I sat without speaking. Then, as the whole idea of being shot at sunk in and with it the relief that we were okay, we both started talking at once.

"Can you believe they missed us?"

"We are so lucky!"

"I wonder if the paintings are damaged."

"Philippe is going to wonder where we are."

"We should call him and let him know we're going to be late."

When Malone got back to the car, it was as if we couldn't stop. He eventually held up his hand to silence us.

"I'm going to have to take your car in and have the forensics team go over it," he explained to April Mae.

"But we have to deliver the cat paintings to the gallery," she protested. "Philippe is expecting us."

"The gallery is going to have to wait for these paintings."

"Are they damaged?" I asked. It would be terrible after all April Mae had gone through to get the cats painting again and things set up with Philippe if she had to start over.

I guess it would be more terrible if the bullets had found their mark.

CHAPTER TWENTY-FOUR

Malone dropped us off at April Mae's, and over a glass of Kitty's wine, we considered the possibilities.

Organized crime involvement sounded more and more promising. But if they had killed Kitty over some investment gone wrong, why would April Mae be a target? It didn't make sense to me.

I still thought there was a good possibility it was someone close to Kitty.

The cats seemed to sense our distress and at first nuzzled our ankles and then eventually insisted on being on the couch with us. Toby draped himself on April Mae's lap, and Minou cuddled against my side. I felt myself relax as I stroked the soft fur. We'd settled in and finally calmed not only the cats but ourselves, when suddenly there was a loud knock.

Pound, pound, pound!

We both jumped.

"I recognize that knock." Though usually it was at my own house. I got up and went to the door to let Malone in.

He followed me into April Mae's living room, where she sat, feet on the coffee table, cat in her lap.

"Ms. Wooben." He nodded, all business. "Your car will be tied up with forensics for a couple of days. I'm not sure when it will be released, but they will call you when they're done."

"Okey-dokey," she responded. "Can you tell who shot at us?"

Of course, he couldn't. This wasn't one of those crime scene television shows, but I understood her need to ask.

"No, I'm afraid I can't." He rubbed his temples. "What I can tell you is that the only reason the two of you are alive is that the Cadillac you bought is armored."

"It's got weapons?" April Mae sat forward dumping poor Tobey on the floor.

"No, it doesn't have weapons. The car is bullet-proof. There are armor plates in the body panels," he explained.

"No way!" April Mae shook her head. "Well, isn't that the bee's knees? I guess I got a good deal on that car."

"I guess you did," I told her. Who'd of thought? The pixie'd inadvertently saved our lives by buying a car that probably *had* belonged to unsavory characters.

"I wanted you to know what was going on with your car." Malone turned to leave. "You may have some challenges getting it repaired. I don't imagine it came from the factory that way. I'll let myself out."

Once Malone was gone, we went back to petting cats and sipping wine and thanking the good Lord for whoever had invented bullet-proof cars.

It was a few days before April Mae got her car back, and when she got it back it was a sight to see in the daylight. I'd never seen something riddled with bullet holes in real life. And to tell you the truth, I hoped I never was that close to one again.

Verdi was a huge hit at the office and soon had things running smoothly. I'd checked in with her to see if she had any questions, but she seemed to intuitively get what each of us needed. She also seemed to understand our clientele was very different. The accountant saw very few people this time of the year. The psychic saw pretty much everyone in her office. I saw no one in my office, and with the real estate agent it varied, depending on where they were in the process.

240

That afternoon, I'd stopped by to get my extra cell phone charger which I'd left on my desk the day before.

"How's it going, Caro?" she asked.

"Great, hon." Just seeing her there made me smile. "How about you?"

"Excellent!" Her burgundy head bobbed. "I wanted to mention to you that while you were out, a Bonnie called, and I believe she may have been the woman you talked to me about. I offered to take her information and have you call, but she was a little skittish. So, I offered her the women's shelter contact number you left, and she took it."

"That's fabulous, Verdi." I was so relieved. I'd stopped by the house in Ruby Point again but couldn't raise anyone, and I'd continued to worry about the woman with the little Yorkie. "I hope she makes contact."

CHAPTER TWENTY-FIVE

April Mae's message on my cell phone sounded frantic, so I drove straight home. I dropped my purse, let Dogbert out for a quick pit stop, and then headed next door.

When April Mae opened the door, she looked like she'd been crying. "The cats are gone," she wailed.

"What?"

"Tobey and Minou. They're gone."

"How? When?" I realized I sounded like I was hitting her with questions, but I couldn't help it. I was in shock.

"I don't know how. I came home from the beauty parlor, and they didn't come out to greet me. They usually do, but not always. So, I called to them and started lookin' all over." I could hear the growing panic in her voice. "Caro, I have looked high and low and in every nook and cranny of this house. They are not here. And they couldn't get out on their own."

"We'd better call Malone."

"Good idea. Why didn't I think of that?"

I dialed Malone's number on my cell phone. I'd added him to my "Top Contacts" so his number was easy to find. I'm not sure what that says about the life I lead that I have a homicide detective as one of my "Top Contacts."

I was so used to his voicemail I didn't realize immediately that he was talking to me.

"Caro? Hello? Are you there?"

"Sorry. Yes, I'm at April's, and the cats are missing."

There was a long pause.

In the pause, where I replayed what I'd just said, I had two thoughts. Briefly, I wondered when I'd started thinking of this as April's house and not Kitty's. The other was how totally inappropriate it was to call a homicide detective with a missing pet report.

"Do you want me to have Sgt. Peterson call you?" he spoke very slowly in his irritating you-are-crazy-as-a-loon voice.

"No, no, I can do that. And I'll call Don Furry at the ARL in case they've been dropped off there. I'm not sure why I called you. It seemed like it might have something to do with the people April's been talking to about Kitty being shot, and you'd asked me to keep an eye on things and let you know."

As soon as I said the words I looked up and saw April's face, and I felt like an incredible heel.

"Detective Malone asked you to keep an eye on me." Her already high pitch went higher. "I thought you were helpin' me, Caro. I thought you were my friend."

CHAPTER TWENTY-SIX

I was still on April Mae's list. Yeah, that list. Again. She'd only just recovered from my turning her into the police for having a gun in her pickup.

I'd apologized for not being totally honest with her, and she'd said she understood, but there was still a hesitance. I didn't blame her. How would anyone feel if someone who claimed to be a friend was really reporting in to the police about them?

I'd said I would go with April Mae to put up flyers offering a reward for the return of Tobey and Minou. The effort was partly in hopes of redeeming myself but mostly because I truly was concerned about the cats.

We'd soon put flyers up in most of the businesses in downtown. At least the ones who were currently open.

Our final stop was Whole Foods. We talked to the store manager who okayed putting the poster on their bulletin board. April Mae took care of tacking up the flyer while I ran inside to get us something to drink. Seemed like we'd been at this for hours. The idea of someone breaking in and taking the cats was crazy but it had to be what happened. I grabbed a couple of sport drinks to rehydrate us and got in the "Less than ten items" line to pay.

Clive, the stuck-on-himself artist, was in front of me. He only had a container of milk. Thank goodness. I really wanted to keep moving.

"Did you get your flyer up?" the cashier asked me.

"My friend is posting it now."

Clive turned to look at me. "Flyer?"

"Yes, Kitty Bardot's cats are missing."

"Too bad." His tone held no sympathy, and I wished he'd move so I could pay.

"I know you don't like the concept of painting cats, but I'd think you'd at least care that the animals are missing." I don't know why I wasted my breath, but I couldn't let his cold attitude pass.

"Oh, I care." His freaky blue eyes were watery and red, and he spoke as if he were congested. The guy seemed to be fighting a cold. Maybe he should be buying orange juice instead of milk. "I'll let you know if I

246

see them."

"Thanks." I handed my money to the cashier and picked up the drinks. Clive moved on without any further words, and I was glad. The guy was so into himself there didn't seem to be any room for empathy for anyone else.

I walked out to the parking lot where April Mae leaned against my car. Her face was flushed, and her usual perkiness was missing. She was taking this really hard.

"Did you see that Clive guy come out?" I handed her one of the sport drinks. "He was in the store."

She shook her head. "Let me guess. He wasn't much interested in helping us find Tobey and Minou."

"You're right." I took a sip, enjoying the cool liquid. "In fact, he was darn right rude."

"I'm not surprised. I ran into him a couple of days ago at the gallery when I was talking to Philippe. He didn't see me at first, 'cause I was playing with Simba." She also paused to take a drink. "He was real ugly about his ideas on animals who created art."

"He was sure clear about his views that day at Franklin's office." I unlocked the car, and April Mae laid the remaining flyers in the back seat.

"He stopped talking when he saw me." April Mae buckled her seatbelt. "I hope Philippe doesn't show any of his new stuff. That's what he was there for, to talk about his new pictures. I think he's nasty."

"Right now, I think he's fighting a nasty cold." I stopped.

Wait a minute. I'd seen those symptoms before. The night of the pet art exhibition. Red-eyes. Sniffly nose. And why was the guy buying milk? He was lactose intolerant. I remembered he'd passed on hors d'oeuvres at the event where we'd met because of the chance there might be cheese in them.

I grabbed April Mae's arm. "I think I know who may have Tobey and Minou."

I filled her in on my thoughts.

We called Malone, reached his voicemail, and left him a message. He called back almost immediately. I imagine because he thought we had information about his murder investigation, and not because he thought we'd cracked the cat-kidnapping case.

April Mae explained what had just happened and filled him in on all the derogatory comments Clive had made about the cats and their painting.

Then I got on the phone and told him again about Clive and his allergies and how he'd acted when I'd talked to him in the grocery store. I also felt it was important to mention he'd bought milk though he himself couldn't tolerate dairy products. Many non-cat-owners assume cats drink milk, while many don't care for it, and some can't tolerate it at all.

Malone did a lot of "uh-huh" and "I see" type comments.

"I'll do what I can." He didn't sound uncaring, but I'd guess when your job is homicide . . . well, you get the idea. "I can send someone to his house. But if he's not cooperative, I doubt we can get a search warrant based on red eyes, a runny nose, and a gallon of milk."

I felt my heart drop. "I understand. Please do what you can."

I disconnected and handed the phone back to April Mae.

"What did he say?"

"He said they'd send someone to Clive's house, but if he wouldn't let them look, they probably wouldn't be able to get a search warrant."

"What?" She sputtered. "But if he's got my cats — he'd better let them in, he'd better give them back."

"They're gonna try, honey." I was trying to stay calm myself. "Malone will do his best. Sgt. Peterson will probably go, and he's plenty burly. I'll bet he'll scare stupid old Clive into confessing and giving him the cats."

"But, but —" April Mae was full-fledged crying now.

Not sad tears, these were mad tears. I recognized them because I'd shed a few of those myself.

"Come on, now, sugar. Hang tight." I unearthed a few tissues from my purse. "We've got to let the police do their job."

I put the car in gear and headed back home. I had every confidence in Malone. I knew he'd do everything he could. I just wished I felt better about what could be done.

I dropped April Mae off and told her I'd check in later.

I had a couple of follow-up appointments. I wanted to check in on any further communication with Bonnie and the women's shelter. And then I planned to call Detective Malone and beg him to do something.

I thought I'd shown tremendous restraint by not driving directly to Clive's house. Okay, I'll admit, I did look up where he lived. His home was high up on the hillside, where the houses hugged the cliffs like barnacles. I wrote down the address.

Chapter Twenty-Seven

Convincing yourself a bad idea is a good one, is a bad idea.

I'd meant my promise to Detective Malone. I really had. I'd said I'd report everything to him.

I'd meant my promise to Sam, too. I'd said I wouldn't take unnecessary chances that might put me in danger.

I'd truly meant both promises.

But in the end things did get out of hand, and I didn't have time to play it safe. It wasn't like I wanted to get involved or take unnecessary chances; I had to protect April Mae.

I got home from the women's shelter where Bonnie and her dog, Bitty, were now settled in and safe. The staff there would work to help Bonnie get back to Illinois, which is what it sounded like she wanted to do.

Happy to be home, I'd walked in the door

and laid my keys and cell phone on the table, when I noticed I had a message. I'd had my cell on vibrate while I'd been at the shelter. When I listened to the message, my heart sank.

April Mae's usually chirpy voice was shaky. "Caro, I know the police can't do anything because they don't have any proof, but I can't just sit here while that jerk has my babies. I'm gonna get some evidence."

I knew she'd gone to Clive's house. Alone.

I could only hope she'd meant she was doing something like watching his house and taking pictures. Not doing something like breaking in.

I picked up my keys and headed back out. It was a winding drive up in the Hills to Clive's place. He was almost in the Top of World section. The roads jogged back and forth to deal with the steep grade.

As I got closer, I kept an eye out for April's car. Within two blocks of Clive's address, I saw the big black Cadillac.

It would have been easy to spot simply because there weren't many cars around like it. Okay, none.

It was even easier to identify because of the bullet holes still visible on the side panel. I pulled up behind it and parked. I hoped she was in the car.

A stakeout, I could handle. Breaking and entering, I would have to call in Malone.

I peered in the windows of the Caddy.

Damn. No April Mae.

I started walking.

As I approached Clive's house, I could see all the lights were off. I kept an eye out as I walked. The little pixie could be hiding in the bushes. The hedges were dense and green. They would give good cover.

I stood across the street, watching. I leaned into the thick scratchy greenery. It was dark enough and the street lights dim enough that I was pretty sure no would spot me.

My eyes adjusted to the darkness, and it wasn't long before I noticed there was a spot of light that bobbed in the backyard. The light stopped near the back of the house.

I remembered April Mae's skill when she'd picked the lock of the display case at the Bow Wow Boutique. Dollars to donuts, Clive's back door would be no problem for her.

I stayed in place. If she got in the house, looked around and either found the cats and got them out, or found they weren't there, all was good. If the cats were there, we'd deal with Clive through the proper channels at the police department. Sgt. Peterson was no Detective Malone, but he was no one to mess with as far as treatment of animals. If Clive had taken Tobey and Minou, he'd have Sgt. Peterson to deal with. And me. And April Mae. He was damn lucky Diana was out of the country.

I saw the light disappear and figured she was in.

Headlights came down the street, and I backed further into the hedge. The silver SUV made a wide turn and pulled into Clive's driveway. I didn't know what Clive drove, but there was no mistaking the figure who climbed out. Dragging his fingers through his shoulder-length hair, he jingled his keys as he walked to the front door.

Holy crap! I had to warn April Mae!

Holy crap! I had to call Malone!

I probably should have called 911, but all I could think of was that I'd told Malone I'd keep an eye on April Mae. Now, she was probably going to be locked up for breaking into Clive's house. There was no way Clive wouldn't press charges. Crap!

There was a chance I could get her out of the house before Clive discovered her.

I hit Malone's number on speed dial. Got his voicemail. Left a message and ran for the back of Clive's property.

Thank goodness when April Mae'd picked the lock she'd left the door open. Probably thinking of a quick get-away for herself rather than a quick entry for me.

The whole back of Clive's house was an enclosed area with windows on three sides. I wasn't sure what it was called in California, but in Texas we call it a back porch. Clive had made it into a studio. It was difficult to see in the dim light, but I looked around as quickly as I could.

At the far end of the studio was a large wire dog crate, and in the crate were Tobey and Minou.

"Meow, meow," they cried in unison.

Dammit. The self-involved nut job did have the cats. April Mae'd been right.

I could hear Clive opening the front door. Humming to himself.

He had no idea we were there. I'd get April Mae, we'd get out, call 911 like I should have done in the first place.

I didn't know how we'd explain we'd seen the cats, but we'd somehow convince the police to come in and get them.

"April Mae," I whispered as loud as I could. "April Mae, it's me, Caro."

"Meow, meooow." Tobey and Minou paced in the big crate and yowled. They could see me and were frantic. I was afraid to open the crate for fear they'd take off. I didn't think I could corral them in time to get out.

"Shhh. Hush now, you two." I carefully made my way to the cats. "We'll get you out of there soon."

The porch suddenly got less dark as Clive began flipping on lights in the other rooms. I leaned back, out of sight I hoped. I could see the whole space and still didn't see April Mae. I didn't want to leave without her, but I was out of time.

"April Mae," I hissed. "Where are you?"

"She's right here." The chilling voice came from right behind me. "But she can't answer right now because she's a little busy."

I spun around to face Clive holding a gun to April's head. "What the hell do you think you're doing?" he asked, his other hand clutching her arm.

A gun? Holy cat scat!

Then it hit me, this was not a simple cat-napping.

Clive was not just a temperamental artist with an ego. A run-of-the-mill narcissist, as I'd thought before. He was a psychopath with a narcissism disorder. The cats were just the cat-alyst, if you'll excuse a bad pun at a time like this.

"Taking care of some loose ends, Ms. Lamont. So nice of you to stop by and make it easy for me." His red eyes, which I knew were a reaction to the cats, burned with menace.

My heart raced in my chest, but I kept my voice steady. "You should know I called the police before I came looking for April Mae."

"Sure you did."

My eyes connected with April's, and I tried to telegraph that I really had. Malone would check his messages, and he would come. What we needed to do was delay for as long as possible.

"Give me back my cats." The blonde pixie was furious.

"I could have done that, and we'd be square. But you had to go snooping through my things, didn't you?"

"I did. But I didn't see nothin'." April Mae was no better at bluffing than I was.

"Right. Okay, come on, you two. We need to get you out of here just in case Miss Beauty Queen here is telling the truth. I'm thinking not, or they would have been here by now."

He still had a fierce grip on April Mae's arm with one hand and held the handgun to her temple with the other hand.

"You jerk." She twisted and turned but couldn't get loose.

"I'm afraid the two off you are going to be found shot. Victims of the Laguna Beach sniper who strikes again." With his gun hand, he reached behind him and pulled what looked like a gun case from the broom closet and slung it over his shoulder. It appeared heavy, so my guess was a rifle.

And since we were all guessing here, I also guessed it was the rifle used to shoot Kitty Bardot.

He'd almost shot us, too, a few days ago. April's crazy purchase of a car from the mob was the only thing that had saved us.

I didn't know where he planned to take us, but I figured we were goners if we left the house. Malone would never know where to look for us. Not until someone found our bodies. Delay was our only chance.

"Why?" I hoped his ego would help me keep him talking.

"Why what?"

"Why kill Kitty?" If he was classic narcissism personality disorder, he wouldn't be able to resist talking about himself. If, and it was a big if, he didn't figure out what I was trying to do.

"Why kill Kitty?" I repeated. "You're obviously a talented artist."

"I am." He flipped on the switch, and spotlights illuminated the canvases around

258

the room. They'd been disturbing in half light. They were scary fully lit.

"We saw your work at Philippe's gallery."

"That was my 'Survival' series." He preened. "This is my 'Rage' series."

Clearly.

Red paint slashed across the canvases. Black lines cut through the red on some. On others the red spattered the space like — like blood.

I swallowed hard. "Why . . . ah . . . Kitty?"

"She wouldn't take me as a client. Said she 'had to be selective' and then when she got all involved with her painting cats, she wouldn't even see me. Threatened to have me thrown out if I showed up at her fancy office."

"There are other publicists."

"But she was the best. I am the best. I didn't want someone else." His head raised along with his voice.

"So you killed her?"

"Philippe was going to do a show for me, but then Kitty talked him into doing a show for her evil cats. Just listen to them."

Tobey and Minou yowled from their cages.

"Then I couldn't paint. When the cats painted." He glared in their direction. "I couldn't. It was as if they'd taken my muse."

I resisted any retort. *Keep talking, buddy.*

Clive smiled. "So Kitty had to go. Simple logic, really."

April looked up at him, and I thought he would fry alive from the fire in her eyes.

We were doing well though. This was taking time.

If we could keep him talking, Malone would come.

I hadn't really thought it through though, because if Malone knocked on his door, he'd just say we weren't there. Malone would have to get a search warrant, and then Clive would still take us off somewhere and kill us.

"Once she was gone," Clive continued, "my muse returned. All was good. This is my best work." He swept his gun toward the canvases. "Until *she* came." His white-knuckle grip on April Mae tightened, and he tapped the gun against her temple.

"Now she's got them painting again. I can't have that."

"What are you going to do with Tobey and Minou?" April bit out.

"Oh, not to worry. I've found a couple who will take them. That's where I was when you broke into my house. They'll take them far away from here and have new homes for them. They'll be fine. The couple are breeders, and they were very impressed that I had special cats. Special cats, but they'll never paint again. They'll just be cats."

"You're giving Tobey and Minou to breeders!"

He smiled. "I know, brilliant isn't it?"

"You low-life, scum bag," April Mae stomped on Clive's foot with her high-heeled boots, and then when he pitched forward she kneed him in the groin.

I grabbed for the handgun and tried to wrestle it out of his hand, but he wasn't going to give up that easily. I kicked him in the shin and wrapped myself around his body. I had height on him. And fear.

He lost his balance and fell. Into a still wet painting.

"Look what you've done!" he shrieked like a banshee.

The destruction of the painting was all the distraction I needed. I grabbed the gun from his slippery hand and crawled away from the knocked-over paintings.

I stood, steadied the weapon and pointed it at Clive who was struggling to his feet. I didn't know if I could shoot him, but I hoped I could. Our lives depended on it.

Just then I heard a metallic slide and a click. April Mae had assembled the rifle and had Clive in her sights.

"Just like a huntin' rifle." She grinned at me. "Don't think I won't shoot you, 'cause I will. It'd be my pleasure."

"She will, too," I told him.

"That won't be necessary." I hadn't heard Malone come in, but it looked like he'd heard enough. His service weapon was also pointed at Clive.

"Caro, are you okay?" Malone's face was pale. Could that be concern?

I looked down at the dark maroon stain on my side, the bright red splotches on my knees, my hands spattered with crimson. I could only imagine what the rest of me looked like.

"It's paint." April actually giggled. It might have been hysteria rather than humor, but as I looked at the red paint all over me, it did look like I was the walking dead.

I snickered too.

Malone looked like he might like to shoot us all.

"Okay, ladies. I've got this." He hand-cuffed Clive and made him sit on the floor. Then he called for backup.

I handed Malone the gun I still held.

April handed over the rifle.

Ignoring the red paint that covered me from head to toe, April Mae hugged me.

The place was soon abuzz with Laguna

Beach police officers, crime scene techs, and it wasn't long before a crowd of news teams collected outside.

April Mae asked if she could take Tobey and Minou home. Malone said she could. He would send an officer by later to take our statements. I didn't think the statement would cover all the explaining I had to do.

He helped us get the cats out of the cage and to the Caddy. Once we'd sent April Mae on her way, he waited while I spread some towels on my car seat before I got in. Most of the red paint was dry, but I didn't want to take any chances.

"Caro . . ." He leaned on the door of the Mercedes.

"Yes?"

"We really do have to stop meeting like this. I think I aged ten years in the last twenty minutes." He shut the car door and walked away.

Chapter Twenty-Eight

The announcement was a work of art in its own right. High-quality paper, enticing graphics, pictures of cute kittens. Always an attention-getter.

Arman Gallery–Mewsings–Saturday 3:00– 7:00 PM

It had taken me more than a week and a professional exfoliation treatment to get the red paint off my skin.

I was so excited for April Mae and her protégées. The showing of Tobey and Minou's latest creations had created quite a stir. Not only was local media covering the event, but there was also national coverage.

April Mae had partnered with the Laguna Beach ARL on the event, and so Don Furry and the other volunteers were to be on hand. Diana Knight had thrown her considerable influence behind the cause, and Franklin had done his PR thing.

I'd decided on a deep green Carolina Herrera. Sleeveless, simple, and of course, accented by Grandma Tillie's brooch. Grey had said he and Mel would be in attendance. Tomorrow I'd make sure the heirloom was where Mel couldn't get her hands on it. And after she saw me with the brooch tonight, I'd make sure the copy was where she'd be sure to find it. I smiled to myself. I loved the double feint. She'd think she had the real one. The real one would be safe. Checkmate.

Sam stepped inside when I answered the door. His expression made me feel like my lengthy preparations had been all worthwhile.

He immediately enveloped me in an embrace, and I melted into him. We'd not seen each other since before Clive's arrest.

"My God, I'm so glad you're safe." This hug was quite a bit different from April Mae's but no less sincere. He also kissed me and said a bunch of things in Greek that I didn't understand. I'm pretty sure they would have scared me if I had.

He finally held me at arm's length, brushed my hair back, and touched my cheek with his knuckles. "Caro, love. You look incredible."

"You look pretty incredible yourself." I laughed to lighten the moment. He did look good. You had to love a guy who could look just as yummy in formal clothes as he did in tennis shorts.

I picked up my evening bag and waved good-bye to Dogbert, Thelma, and Louise who watched from the couch. "Bye, kids, keep an eye on things while I'm gone." They were so darn cute and looked like they understood every word.

"Bye." Sam also waved at them.

The chariot . . . ah . . . Ferrari was in the drive.

It was a perfect clear fall evening, and the drive, though short, gave us a brief glimpse of the breaking waves and the endless blue where it was kissed by the rim of fire as the sun cashed out on the day. I sighed. All was right in my world.

When we arrived at the Arman Gallery, the place was packed. Philippe had done a great job of displaying Tobey and Minou's paintings. The press was treating the gallery showing like a red carpet event.

Franklin had promoted the showing beyond expectations. Kitty would have been proud of him. He had proved to be brilliant. Whether he would continue with the agency, now to be called Chesney PR, and just be a weekend goat herder, or whether he'd pack it all in and raise fainting goats full time, who knew?

I spotted him across the room talking to Philippe. April Mae had dressed up for the occasion; her Bengal cat hairdo had been smoothed, tamed, and sprayed in place. It perfectly matched her fur-patterned dress. She was entertaining a group of reporters with stories of how the cats got their inspiration.

Diana Knight and Dino Riccio were back and talking with Teri, the Laguna Beach mayor. Diana was lovely in a new wine-colored Valentino frock. A nod to her recent trip to Italy, no doubt.

I'd missed her. I made my way through the crowd to her side.

"Don't you look nice." I kissed her on the cheek. "I take it you enjoyed your trip."

"It was incredible, Caro. You have to see my photos. Well, I won't bore you with all of them, but you have to see some of them."

"I'd love to."

"And you," she grinned. "Another murder solved. You are a sensation. See, I was right, the police need your expertise."

"I didn't solve this one. It sort of solved itself."

"But you saved the day. Or saved the cats, I guess it would be." She laughed.

"I'm glad it all worked out." I looked

around the gallery. I thought of the relief Kitty's killer was behind bars. How thrilled she would've been at the cats' success. But also how it had worked out for Verdi, and especially for Bonnie and her little dog, who were now safe. And for April Mae who was across the room, hugging everyone in sight.

"How fun is this?" Diana followed my gaze around the room. "Quite the crowd, and Kitty's sister has turned out to be a strong supporter for the rescue." She noted Don Furry and others from the Laguna Beach Animal Rescue.

Sam appeared with glasses of champagne for us all.

He held his crystal flute high in a toast. "To friends, family, and felines."

I touched my glass to his and then to Diana's. "Yes, to friends, fam—" Before I could finish, I heard Diana gasp.

I turned to see what had drawn her attention and as if in slow motion I noted my cousin, Melinda, and her fiancé, Grey, step through the press line at the front of the gallery.

Mel looked striking in black. Her dark hair was pulled back and accented her classic to-die-for cheekbones, her skin was flawless as always, her posture perfection. The little black dress, if I wasn't mistaken, was Gianni

Versace, but it wasn't the dress I was interested in.

Perched on the shoulder of the perfect little black dress was Grandma Tillie's brooch.

I looked down at the brooch pinned to my shoulder.

She spotted me, and her gaze landed on the brooch I wore.

We made eye contact.

We both had the brooch.

The question was now which one of us had the real one and which one had the fake.

RECIPES

YAPPY HOUR PUPCAKES
(Served by Mel & Darby at their Yappy Hour event)

You'll need the following ingredients:

2 carrots, grated
2 ripe bananas, mashed
1 egg
3 cups water
1/2 teaspoon vanilla
2 tablespoons honey
4 cups flour
1 teaspoon baking powder
1 teaspoon nutmeg
1 teaspoon cinnamon

Preheat your oven to 350 degrees.

Line a cupcake tin with festive dog-themed cupcakes papers.

Blend water, carrots, egg, vanilla and honey in a big bowl. Then add the mashed bananas.

In another bowl, blend the flour, baking powder, nutmeg and cinnamon.

Add the flour mix to the first (carrot/egg) mixture and blend them together thoroughly.

Spoon the mixture into the cupcake papers.

Bake the pupcakes for 30 minutes. Times can vary depending on your oven so it's a good idea to test the pupcakes by inserting a toothpick in the middle. If it comes out clean, your pupcakes are done.

Frosting is optional, but if you want to add frosting here's a quick idea.

2 tablespoons plain yogurt
2 tablespoons honey
1 package (6 oz.) cream cheese

Mix the ingredients together until smooth, frost the cooled pupcakes, and serve.

Caro's Homemade Kitty Cookies

This recipe uses shredded chicken (don't tell Walter) but you can use beef or fish, if your cat prefers it.

You'll need the following ingredients:

1-1/2 cups of cooked chicken, shredded into small pieces
1 cup of whole wheat flour
1/2 cup of chicken broth
1/3 cup of cornmeal
1 teaspoon of margarine, softened

Preheat your oven to 350 degrees

Mix the chicken, margarine, and chicken broth in a bowl. Then add the cornmeal and flour.

Knead the dough into a ball and roll it out to about 1/4 inch in thickness.

Cut into one inch pieces and place on an ungreased cookie sheet. Bake for 20 minutes and let cool.

This recipe makes 18–24 cookies.

Remember, these treats contain no preserva-

tives and so unlike commercial treats, you
need to make sure to store them with that
in mind.

Caro recommends refrigerating unused por-
tions and labeling them with the date they
were made.

ACKNOWLEDGEMENTS

As always, a big thank-you to our families for their sacrifices. We know you love us because you give so much so we can pursue our dreams.

Also, a huge thanks to our writing families. Our critique group, IRN, PAL of Central Iowa, Sisters in Crime, Mystery Writers of America, the Kiss of Death, RWA, and the many supportive online groups.

We are constantly awed by the supportive team at Bell Bridge Books. You are awesome to work with and it goes without saying these are better books and we are better writers because of your efforts.

And, finally, to our readers. You rock! Your notes, your emails, your comments. We are so blessed to hear from so many of you and it makes it all worthwhile.

We love to hear about your pets, we love to hear from you! Thank-you for taking the time to write to us.

ML & Anita aka Sparkle Abbey
www.SparkleAbbey.com

ABOUT THE AUTHORS

Sparkle Abbey is the pseudonym of two mystery authors (Mary Lee Woods and Anita Carter). They are friends and neighbors as well as co-writers of the Pampered Pets Mystery Series. The pen name was created by combining the names of their rescue pets — Sparkle (Mary Lee's cat) and Abbey (Anita's dog). They reside in central Iowa, but if they could write anywhere, you would find them on the beach with their laptops and depending on the time of day, with either an iced tea or a margarita.

Mary Lee

Mary Lee Salsbury Woods is the "Sparkle" half of Sparkle Abbey. She is past-president of Sisters in Crime–Iowa and a member of Mystery Writers of America, Romance Writers of America, Kiss of Death, the RWA Mystery Suspense chapter, Sisters in Crime, and the SinC Internet group Guppies.

Prior to publishing the Pampered Pet Mystery series with Bell Bridge Books, Mary Lee won first place in the Daphne du Maurier contest, sponsored by the Kiss of Death chapter of RWA, and was a finalist in Murder in the Grove's mystery contest, as well as Killer Nashville's Claymore Dagger contest.

Mary Lee is an avid reader and supporter of public libraries. She lives in Central Iowa with her husband, Tim, and Sparkle the rescue cat namesake of Sparkle Abbey. In her day job she is the non-techie in the IT Department. Any spare time she spends reading and enjoying her sons and daughters-in-law, and four grandchildren.

Anita

Anita Carter is the "Abbey" half of Sparkle Abbey. She is president of Sisters in Crime–Iowa and a member of Mystery Writers of America, Romance Writers of America, Kiss of Death, the RWA Mystery Suspense chapter, and Sisters in Crime.

She grew up reading Trixie Belden, Nancy Drew and the Margo Mystery series by Jerry B. Jenkins (years before his popular Left Behind Series.) Her family is grateful

all the years of "fending for yourself" din-
ners of spaghetti and frozen pizza have
finally paid off, even though they haven't
exactly stopped.

In Anita's day job, she works for a staffing
company. She also lives in Central Iowa
with her husband and four children, son-in-
law, grandchild and three rescue dogs,
Abby, Chewy and Sophie.